ANY SMALL THING
CAN SAVE YOU

BLUEHEN BOOKS

A MEMBER OF PENGUIN PUTNAM INC.

New York

ANY
SMALL THING
CAN
SAVE YOU

A BESTIARY

CHRISTINA
ADAM

BlueHen Books
a member of
Penguin Putnam Inc.
375 Hudson Street
New York, NY 10014

Library of Congress Cataloging-in-Publication Data

Adam, Christina.
Any small thing can save you : a bestiary / Christina Adam.
        p.   cm.
        ISBN 0-399-14814-0
1. Human-animal relationships—Fiction.   2. Animals—Fiction.
                    I. Title.
PS3601.D36 A8   2001   2001035464
            813'.54—dc21

Printed in the United States of America
1 3 5 7 9 10 8 6 4 2

This book is printed on acid-free paper. ∞

Book design by Marysarah Quinn

For my brother and sister

and

Jama Laurent

Any small thing can save you.

Because the golden egg gleamed

in my basket once, though my childhood

became an immense sheet of darkening water,

I was Noah, and I was his ark,

and there were two of every animal inside me.

MARK DOTY, *"Ararat"*

ANY SMALL THING
CAN SAVE YOU

ASP

When she taught Latin in high school, her students had performed an elaborate skit that ended with the death of Cleopatra, stung by an asp. The cast found every opportunity and application for the word "asp," with Milton-like s's—that soft susurrus—hissing out into the audience, held as long as possible before the final p. Twenty years later, Helena still laughed to think of where, *anatomically speaking,* the Latin club had located the fatal strike, but in fact, she was terrified of snakes. When she and her husband had fixed fences on the ranch, this was the one thing she found comforting: At that altitude, there were no snakes. It was never necessary, even in tall grass and weeds, to watch where they were going.

When they retired and moved south to New Mexico, the neighbors cautioned them not to water at night, a practice that brought snakes down from the desert. They were to watch for the wedge-shaped head of a rattler, and listen for the dry, warning sound. She had planted a garden in the unfamiliar soil that seemed like gumbo to her, a soil she doubted would grow anything. They built *houses* with this soil, hers in particular. She planted the most common flowers: marigolds and zinnias, flowers that, in the mountains, had turned black at the slightest threat of frost, that seemed to call to frost and bring it down. In New Mexico, she planted her first tomato. "Before I die," she thought, "I want to eat a ripe tomato, still warm from hanging on the vine." She wanted to grow strawberries, and peaches—fruits she could remember having taste and sweetness when she was a girl.

She tried to persuade Stan to help her dig manure into the beds around the house, to amend the heavy soil and make it friable, but it was all she could do to get him to help water. Grudgingly, he sprinkled and cut the lawn. He had started a small business and spent his days sitting in his underwear at a large, pale gray computer in his den. Piles of paper grew around him and slithered to the floor. He went for days without shaving. He was enthralled by technology, and she had to admit, he was happy. A rancher all his life, he told her, "I've seen all the dirt I ever want to see."

The tile floors aggravated Helena's arthritis to the point that there were nights she couldn't sleep. Still, she took pleasure in the coming of spring, the smooth floors remaining cool in the advancing heat. When she left the darkened house to step outside, she understood for the first time what people meant when they said "blazing heat." The sun was such a bright assault that, as she first walked into the yard, she saw darkened images at the edge of her field of vision. They followed her back indoors, like shapes left in the air by flashbulbs.

She began to garden in the evenings, when the sun had passed behind the height of the willow trees that bounded their yard. She wore shorts and sleeveless blouses and walked among the flowers in her bare feet, pulling weeds. Large toads appeared, buried up to their eyes in the damp mud, or jumping just ahead of her as she watered. Bullfrogs took up a drumming in the ditch across the road, so loud, she thought, they must be the size of kettle drums. She went so far as to think of stringing lights, that she might garden into the night.

As summer advanced, the heat rose up through her feet even in the evening. It forced her to stop weeding and walk indoors to cool herself. That day, she'd been thinking about the sadness of gardening. How the act itself was about waiting. She thought it was too late for her to plant a tree. She entered the kitchen and started for the sink. Looking down, she saw a long, green snake, so rounded and perfect—so still—she thought, "It's a rubber snake; Stan is playing a trick on me." She looked more closely, her eyes adjusting to the dim light. A swift, forked tongue, like a felt tab, flicked out.

Slowly she backed away. She could see Stan out the window, intent on some business, but she couldn't call to him or she would frighten off the snake. She crossed the kitchen, waving her arms, but he couldn't see. He was watering shrubs as he disappeared around the corner of the house. She didn't call until she stepped out the back door, but even then, he didn't hear.

She shouted, "Stan!" and he glanced up. *"What?"* he said, with such an edge of irritation in his voice, she stopped still. She had wanted him to come back with her to see the snake, how green and perfect it was and how unexpected, because it was round and of a substance different from the things that belong inside a house. But his tone knocked the wind out of her. She said, "There's a snake in the kitchen."

He dropped the hose and strode toward the door, demanding, "What kind of snake is it? Is it poisonous?" She followed. "No," she said. "It has a pointed head; I don't think it's poisonous."

By the time they returned to the kitchen, the snake had slithered along the cupboards to the opposite corner. Stan looked at it and said, "Wait here; I'll go get something." He disappeared into his den, and she could hear him shuffling boxes. While she watched, the snake nosed up into the exact corner *between* the cupboards and in an instant disappeared, as if it had been sucked up by a vacuum tube.

When Stan returned with a large, black file box, she tried to explain where the snake had gone, and how quickly. Stan produced a flashlight and began to remove pots and pans.

"No," she said, "he's not in there. He went up *between* the cupboards."

Stan was not listening.

"Just leave it," she said. "Let's turn off the lights and set out a pan of water. Maybe the snake will come out on its own."

Stan continued to pull out pots, setting them down on the kitchen floor. She pictured herself having to put them all back, the arthritis in her hip and knees sharp with every bend. Suddenly furious with him, she filled a shallow pan with water and set it on the rug before the sink. She found herself demanding, in a voice she scarcely recognized,

"*Why?* Why don't you listen to me?"

He stopped removing pans and stared at her. In silence, she went ahead and fixed herself the glass of ice water she had come inside for in the first place, carried it across the open room to the couch, and sat down with her back to the kitchen. It was too late now to retreat outside, and too soon to go to bed. Trapped in her own house, because she didn't want to talk to Stan, she watched the last light of the sunset fade to gray.

Mud was drying on her bare feet, pulling the skin taut in a way she could recall from summer nights in her childhood. Her feet just lightly touched the floor. She heard Stan shuffle back to his study, and she thought of the snake. How had she known it wasn't poisonous? It had a head the shape of a finger, of an animal's penis. She laughed to herself, thinking that the snake was still behind her in the kitchen, and she ought to pick up her feet. Go wash them and tuck them underneath her. She thought of it but didn't move. She thought of saying to the neighbors, "And then, the worst thing you can imagine happened, your worst nightmare . . ." and still, she didn't lift her feet. Reasonably, she thought it would be hours before the snake ventured out of the cupboard.

She felt her anger at Stan leave with the heat of the day, as if evaporating from her skin. And then came the touch. The coolest, simplest touch to the back of her heel. Slowly she stood up. The snake looped just in front of the couch and curled away. She circled around it, into the tile foyer, and opened the wide front door. She tried to approach the snake from behind, as if she could herd it, but it turned and came toward her. She stepped toward the snake, and it curved away. Slowly, and by indirect direction, they made progress toward the door. The snake lifted its head slightly, aware of the cool night, a sudden breeze, and like a compass needle shivering and hunting for true north, made its way over the threshold and out onto the porch. Helena closed the door.

She wanted to go tell Stan how, amazingly, she had no fear of the snake, none at all. She felt honored, in fact, by the touch, by the timorous, cool touch of the snake on her heel. She went into the bathroom to wash and change into night-clothes, wondering what she would say to Stan when he came in to bed. Whether to tell him about the snake or not—such a small decision. It would be only one moment in so many of their years together, yet she knew. It would make all the difference in the world.

BAT

After Judith died, it seemed to Raymond he must be the only single man in Carlsbad. Everybody knew a woman—a cousin, a sister, a neighbor—he should meet. He'd been offered so many blind dates, he was threatening to buy a cup of pencils and a cane. Which was the only reason he agreed to help the young biologist spend his evenings banding Mexican swallows. Spring was not far off, and the birds were ready to migrate south.

Barry picked him up after dinner in a new, sparkling white Suburban with the university logo painted on the door, and they drove southwest into the desert, leaving the highway and climbing up through a narrow canyon. Cuts on either side exposed ancient, volcanic action, layers of sedimentary rock jutting at odd angles.

They parked as the sun hovered over the western horizon, hoisted the equipment, and began to hike to the mouth of the cave. Out of shape and out of breath, Raymond remembered that he didn't actually like Barry, who occupied a desk in the construction office preparing an impact paper on a piece of land Raymond hoped to sell to the county. So far, the biologist hadn't located any endangered species, but he wasn't finished looking. Still, Raymond had to hand it to the kid. When the crew gave him a bad time about hunting for "stones and bones" and "bugs and bunnies," Barry only grinned and said, "It's a living."

"The swallows," Barry explained, "leave the cave first, just at sundown." He stationed Raymond at one end of the net, and together, they stretched it lengthwise and braced it in position.

The birds were small and backlit by the sun. Each one, as it struck the net, was briefly stunned, and Barry would cup it in his hand to attach a tiny, silver leg band. The entire process took only a few minutes and Barry was waving at him to lower the net.

"Where do they go?" Raymond asked him.

"At night?" Barry asked.

"No, when they migrate."

"Nobody knows."

"What do you mean, nobody knows?"

Barry shook his head and shrugged. "That's what we're trying to find out."

Raymond helped roll and pack the net, careful that it didn't catch and tear on scrub and cactus barbs. "We don't know," he kept thinking to himself. "We know the exact location of every wolf and grizzly bear in North America, every California condor, but we don't know where these god-damned little birds go." Something about that disturbed him.

"How long?" he asked Barry. "How long before you guys find out?"

Barry laughed. "It doesn't exactly work that way," he said. "There aren't many people working on it. Could take years. Or we might never know."

The sun had dipped past the edge of the western desert and the loss of heat was palpable, as if the sun had been a space heater moved into another room. They left their equipment and hiked a hundred yards to the north. Barry placed his hands on Raymond's shoulders and turned him to face the mouth of the cave.

The smell of guano was almost overpowering, the ammonia bringing tears to his eyes. Barry demonstrated how he should hold his arms out straight from his shoulders, then he stepped away and took up the same position himself.

"Whatever you do," he said, "don't move; as long as you don't move, they won't hit you."

The great gray swarm left the mouth of the cave and in the near darkness swept toward them. It was all Raymond could do to keep still. He was startled and ashamed by how strong the urge to run became. He planted his feet as if his boots were anchored in cement.

Suddenly he was in a wind made of bats. Movement surrounded him, passing over his bare arms the way air flows over the wing of a plane and holds it in the sky. Thousands of bats flew past him, and the sound of wings and the squeals of sonar shimmered in the air. Not a single bat touched his skin.

Raymond hung in the thick, black air, his arms out-
stretched like Jesus on the cross. Oh, he wished Judith were
here, to tell her how, for just this moment, everything he felt
and saw was *working*, humming with a fine precision. He *felt*
like Jesus, gazing out over the multitudes, a man with a
secret so huge, it seemed to him unbearable.

CAT

My husband enjoys bookstores, especially when they specialize in maps and atlases, but I could tell he'd had enough shopping. He stood a little apart while I waited for the clerk to scan the titles on her screen, and without looking at him, I felt the subtle shift in his posture. I heard him sigh.

"That's all right," I said to the clerk. "I'll order the book another time."

I nodded at Jim, and we began to thread our way through the narrow aisles and out onto the street.

Evening had come, and with it, a cooling breeze off the ocean. The street was closed to traffic and the atmosphere was festive, as if release from the day's heat had created a collective sense of lightness and reprieve. An old man with a large, pearlescent accordion stood just outside the bookstore, belting a song into a microphone. His voice was so grating and his singing so off-key, I winced, and looked at Bill, who shook his head and picked up his pace.

Despite the singer's awful voice, I loved his being there. I loved strolling after dark, among crowds of strangers. It felt to me as if we had traveled to Rio instead of Los Angeles. As if we were world travelers, not an ordinary couple on business. I couldn't seem to see enough, to take in enough. I resisted the thought of returning to our hotel room.

We live in a small town in Idaho where I know everyone. When people ask where we come from, they want to know the nearest city. I have to say Boise, but even Boise isn't near, and there's no place to shop, really, even after you get there. The only thing our town is known for is the earthquakes. Which is what we were doing in Los Angeles. My husband and I sell insurance.

Out of the corner of my eye, I saw a shimmering flash of ruby sequins. I stopped and stood on tiptoe. A sign in glittering script arched over a box draped in cloth. It read, "Psychic Cat." I couldn't help but laugh. "Only in Los Angeles," I thought. I wanted to get closer. The sign attracted me the way a jeweled tiara might attract my youngest girl.

Although I knew it would annoy him, I tugged on the sleeve of Jim's jacket until, reluctantly, he followed. A man with black, Prince Valiant hair sat on a stool in the center of the street. Acrobats performed so close they ended long tumbling runs just inches from his stool, yet he showed no sign of alarm. On the cloth-draped box in front of him, two large cats reposed in baskets. Each cat was outfitted in a different, elaborate velvet costume, complete with lace ruffles and headgear. I couldn't quite figure out what was going on. I had to kneel in the street to ask the man. His skin was gray-brown, actually swarthy, and his clothes and hands were dark with dirt and grease. His eyes were the blackest I have ever seen, and a large mole, just where a beauty mark would be, darkened his chin. When he spoke, it was in broken English with a heavy accent, and I realized he was a gypsy.

"What do the cats do?" I asked him.

"Choose a cat. She will tell your fortune."

"How much does it cost?"

He shrugged and said disdainfully, "This is between you and the cat."

I couldn't help myself. I pointed to the cat he called Nostradama. The gypsy produced a can of cat food and a spoon and fed the cat a mouthful, whereupon she rose up on her haunches, her paws in the air. He held up a tray of his own manufacture, built on the order of a toothpick dispenser. When he extended this toward the cat, she stretched out her paw and pressed down on a bar, releasing a small, pink roll of paper. He fed the cat again from the spoon, and she extracted the paper and held it between her paws. I looked around for Jim, so delighted with this performance, I wanted to be sure that he had seen, but his face was impassive.

I started to rise, but the gypsy nodded for me to hold out my hand. I extended a palm, and the cat dropped into it the rolled, pink fortune.

"Thank you!" I said, surprised to find myself addressing the cat, not the man.

I reached into my skirt pocket and found two dollar bills, which I offered to the gypsy. He shook his head, impatient with my slowness, and pointed to the cat, though after she pawed the money softly from my fingers, he was quick to take it from her.

I didn't read the fortune then. Jim had stood watching the acrobats and refused to take any part in the fortune-telling, but I couldn't get over it.

"Weren't they amazing?" I said.

"I'm surprised somebody hasn't called the SPCA," Jim said. "The cats looked sick."

"They looked okay to me," I said.

"Their eyes were runny," Jim said.

I had missed that. I hadn't seen.

"Well," I said, "at least they are well fed."

I still resisted the thought of going back to our hotel room, but I doubted I could talk Jim into stopping in the lobby for a drink. We'd been in meetings all day and I knew he was tired. He preceded me into our room and switched on the TV. I don't know why, but instead of calling home first thing, I took myself into the bathroom to read the fortune. I sat down on the closed lid of the toilet, the automatic fan whirring in my ears. The pink paper was rolled so tightly I

had to hold it open with the fingers of both hands. It had
been typed with so many mistakes and strikeovers, it was dif-
ficult to read. Deciphered, it seemed to say:

> *Season coming up will be one of your most exciting. You
> could show out perform due to financial matters. If not
> all legacy at least part of it will be your. It may appear
> to be more actually than it on the sur-face.*
>
> *Oh! I love you—Wizard.*

It was nonsense. But I let it curl back into its tidy shape and
tucked it into the recesses of my wallet, as if it were a precious memento. Though it came to me at random, I thought,
"This is uniquely mine, and whatever meaning it may have
will be for me to say." I felt ridiculous, but I also thought,
"Animals know things." I remembered a cat we'd had when
we were first married. Before we had the children, Jim had
surprised me with a tiny handful of a silver kitten. How
could I have forgotten her? For the life of me, I couldn't think
of her name, or what had become of her as a grown cat, but
I remembered our first earthquake, the big one in 1983.

Though she was still a kitten, she woke me in the middle of the night. I heard her first, then found her pacing up and down in a line alongside the bed, mewling. Just after that, the floor began to shift, lurching so far left and right, it threw us out of bed. I thought the whole top floor was *sliding* down into the neighbor's yard, and I remember thinking calmly, "This is it. The end. There's nothing we can do." As if in a dream, I didn't think of Jim or of the kitten. I was right there at the moment of my death. I could almost see my body from without, my limbs so supple then, and white. I felt both young and wise—so *present* and alive.

I stood, washed my hands, and emerged from the bathroom. Jim had removed his jacket and pants and propped himself up in the bed, a glass of vodka in one hand, the TV remote in the other. He switched from picture to picture, cutting off loud, urgent voices.

"I'm going out," I said.

"Are you sick?" he asked me. "You want me to go to the drugstore?"

"No," I said. I had the key in one hand, my purse by the handle. "I'm just going out."

He started to get up, and I opened the door. "Call the kids," I said.

In the hallway, I breathed a great sigh of relief. "Oh, thank you wizard!" I couldn't wait to get back in the open air.

Striding down the hallway, I thought of the pink paper in my wallet, of how quickly it rolled back up each time I tried to spread it open. To spring closed like that, it must have been typed and rolled years ago. The gypsy must have packed it in its box each evening, and carried it back home at night . . . to where? Not near here, where rents would be so high. In my mind, I saw the vast and teeming city all around me, strange neighborhoods and alleyways.

Out on the street, I saw the night sky above the buildings glowing, luminous and pink. Still air from the desert held in it, suspended, the smell of jungle flowers and exhaust fumes. Young couples jostled past me on the street and smiled, actually smiled at me. I thought, we are in complicity. We're all hoping. We're all waiting. We're all thinking, "This is *earthquake* weather."

DOVE

Just as I stepped out my front door, I heard an echoing
boom and looked over the adobe wall that divides us
from our neighbor's farm in time to see a dove fall from
the sky. Shivering, my husband's aging dog collided
with the backs of my knees, and I nearly fell. Terrified
of gunshots, she had been trying to crawl into the
kitchen cabinet on top of the pots and pans since the
first day of dove season. I had made a bed for her in
the closet, but she wouldn't leave my side.

The hunters had been out in the corn stubble all

week. Because of the lay of the land, the placement of the buildings and adobe walls, the shots boomed and echoed as if fired from only a few feet away, from inside our own yard. My husband had flown to Washington, D.C., to lobby senators, and I tried to stay indoors during the day. But the gunshots continued into the hour after sunset.

Although we were not young, we were newly wed, in only our second year in that house on four acres, our first house together. We had inherited bullet holes in two of the front windows, and during our first year—our first dove season—I had asked my husband if there wasn't something we could do. Was it legal to shoot so close to houses? My husband shook his head. A long-lapsed Southern Baptist, he said in his wry way, "If I recall correctly . . . it was *God* gave them dominion."

In the spring of that first year, I had begun to repair and paint the tumbledown guest house at the rear of our property. I'd been scraping and sanding all day before I looked up and saw a gray dove nesting just above my head on the long, tapering limb of a willow tree. The tree itself grew on the other side of the wall, but most of the branches swept low over the remains of a small garden in front of the guest house.

The bird nested barely a foot from the top of my head,

and all the time I'd been shifting around, making noise, she hadn't moved at all. As I watched her, she never blinked her round, dark eye, and her slender, black beak curved in the exact shape of her swelling breast.

I was so surprised by her aplomb, I went searching for my husband, and the two of us stood near the tree, observing her. She saw us, but she never stirred. In the following days, she scarcely left the nest. Once, as I was watering, I forgot her altogether and nearly doused her with the hose. I found myself apologizing to the bird. "Whoops, so sorry." Green caterpillars sheared perfect scallops in the leaves of new wisteria, and aphids turned the roses sticky, but I couldn't spray insecticide so close to the bird.

A few days later, I saw two heads with round, dark eyes in the nest. The following day there were three, but I could hardly tell because the nest itself was small, and the mother bird nearly covered the babies, though they were nearly half her size.

I worried when a carpenter arrived to build a Spanish porch on the front of the guest house—but the birds ignored his pounding hammer and the high, incessant whining of his saw.

"Aren't they the rarer kind?" he asked me. "The kind with no white stripe on the wing?"

I didn't know one kind of dove from another except that as a girl I had called these "morning" doves because I always saw them, their feathers shimmering with a pale iridescence, as I walked to school. Now of course I knew they were mourning doves, named for their melancholy song, a lilting *hoo . . . hoo hoo.*

That first year, only our most distant neighbor shot doves when the season came. He drove his teenaged son out to his property south of ours and shot birds on the weekends. I kept the dog inside and tried to comfort her, but only when I held her trusting head in my lap and squeezed her long, bony torso between pillows did she stop shaking. I abandoned work on the guest house.

I never asked him to, but I wanted my husband to stop the shooting. I wanted him to go to the neighbor and force him to stop. But my husband has a policy about these things. Together, we had lived in the country only a short time, but he had spent his childhood on a ranch, and he held with his father's dictum, "Never mess with another man's horses."

·   ·   ·

The day I stood at my front door with the shivering dog, our second autumn in New Mexico, the hunters had been coming nearly every day to shoot in the cornfields north of our house. Buckshot actually pinged off the tin roof of our neighbor's shed, just across the wall. I had waited so long to move out of the city, to live in a house with a yard. I had believed I would never again suffer pounding stereos or barking dogs, traffic noise or neighbors screaming at their children. I'd survived eight years in Washington, and all I wanted was to rest. Every shot made me cringe with fury.

I knew it was unfair to want my husband to stop it. Every day I struggled with myself. Why didn't *I* go stop them? I would intend to; I would grow angrier and angrier, then sink, defeated. What could I actually do? But on the day I stepped out on the porch and heard that first echoing blast, I decided I had to try.

I pulled on a jacket over my T-shirt and laced up heavy boots, though it was only September and very warm. After I latched our gate against the dog and turned down the road, I saw the hunters had parked their pickup on the far side of the neighbor's field. At first, the setting sun—a wall of burning orange—flared so hot behind them, they appeared as chiaroscuro reapers—charcoal figures holding sticks—but as I approached, I made out two men and shotgun barrels. One stood in the corn stubble calling to the other, "On your right! Two o'clock!"

A wary, impatient look on his face, the man nearest the truck lowered the barrels of his shotgun. At his feet, the sandy road was littered with dead birds thrown down at any angle, their wings broken in such sad and wasteful parodies of flight, I wanted to scream at him, "What the hell do you think you're doing?"

Instead I asked him, "Could you possibly move a little farther from the houses?"

He stared at me, a clean-shaven, younger man with a slightly swollen jaw, his hair neatly combed.

"Would it be possible for you to move on down the field, farther away?" I indicated with my arm the fields that ran for miles north along the irrigation ditch.

"We have permission to shoot here . . . right up to the sheds."

"Well," I said, "you wouldn't realize it, but the echo makes it sound as if you're shooting right in my backyard."

I could feel him begin to give, his posture relaxing.

"Well I suppose," he offered.

"Thank you," I said, and turned to walk home. Just as I did, he said, "Ma'am, you won't mind if we just get these few last more . . ." and swung the barrels of his gun back to the sky. It was a boy's reaction. An instinct. Much like a house cat who freezes and turns wild at the sight of a wounded bird.

My boots suddenly too heavy, I retreated back along the road and quietly slipped through the gate, trailing a hand to greet the worried dog. As I turned to go inside, a dove suddenly left the ground and, trying to gain height, flew right into my hands. It felt as if someone had made a soft toss to a child. The dog leaped up and whined, scrambling to climb over me to get to the dove. I closed the bird in my hands and ran back to the guest house, slamming the garden gate behind me. My palms were sweating, and I couldn't believe a bird could generate so much heat. When I reached the old chicken coop behind the guest house, I turned the dove over, searching for wounds. Near one leg, her feathers had clumped together with a yellowish dampness, but I saw no blood. The dog howled, trying to climb the fence and I rushed to find the bird a bowl of water.

As I ran back to the gate for the dog, I saw another bird fall as if in a cartoon—the *boom* of the shotgun, and a child's drawing of a bird, a small, black "m," dropped from the sky—and I thought I would go crazy.

That night I lay awake thinking, "Small potatoes. What do people do who hear gunfire all night? Do they move? How long can you keep moving?"

In the morning, the wounded dove was dead. She had made her way into the very corner of the coop, and on the sandy bottom, bowed her head. Her wings were folded neatly in a compact, perfect package, as if she were presenting herself to God.

The hunters moved on, but that weekend, the neighbor and his son reappeared. I couldn't bring myself to step outside even to water the wilting garden or the brittle grass. The dog, big as she was, managed to scramble all the way into the kitchen cabinet.

When my husband returned from his latest trip—this time to Sante Fe—I told him I couldn't stand it. "Maybe we should move," I said.

We stood in front of the guest house. The work had not progressed as far as I had hoped, since I'd been hiding from the guns. I asked my husband, "Why? There are so many doves, and they are so placid. So unafraid." That's when my husband told me that the neighbor, driving past with his son, had stopped to talk to him.

"He mentioned he might shoot some doves and would we mind," my husband said.

"What did you say?"

"Well, it took me by surprise. I didn't say a thing." He shrugged. "What do you say to a man with a gun?"

When my husband, a large handsome man, a slow-talking, loose-limbed Texan, lobbied for Democratic causes—education, housing for the poor—he was relentless, tough as nails. But he once surprised me by escorting a spider out the door. As a boy, he hunted with his dad, but he hasn't touched a gun since then. We are nearly the same height; made for each other, bone and brain.

In the following weeks, I went searching through the bookshelves for a Bible, but the only one I could find rendered the passage I was looking for into bland Baptist lingo. "Turtle" became "turtle dove." I had to drive to the library to find the King James Version:

For, lo, the winter is past,
the rain is over and gone;
The flowers appear on the
earth; the time of the singing of
birds is come, and the voice of
the turtle is heard in our land.

The year before, when only one neighbor brought his son to shoot doves, I was afraid to ask him to stop. He was a chain-smoking redneck, a recovered drinker with opinions. On each of the few occasions he had stopped to speak to me, he'd managed to work in a slur on Mex'cans. At the time I told myself, "It's better to endure this for a few weeks than to start a war that might last years."

But after my husband told me what he himself had done—when I realized he could have stopped the shooting, *even for one year,* but did not—something fell away. The love I felt for him was changed. I couldn't stop the neighbor or the men who came day after day to shoot doves in the corn-fields. I even came to understand that years of drought and hunting had diminished other predators, hawks and bobcats and coyotes. Something had to be done about the profusion of doves. I never lied to myself. I wasn't any braver than my husband; I spoke to a man with a gun—and said almost nothing. It isn't fair, but we all want something more from our lovers—they must be better than we are.

That second hunting season seemed interminable, but it finally passed. We finished the guest house during the following winter, long months of drought, and came to our third spring in the country. It rained, and the irrigation ditches filled with courting bullfrogs. Red-winged blackbirds called in the twilight, their three-note song as clear as dropping water. In every willow tree, the leaves unfurled, lettuce green, and nesting doves sang in the fading light. Partial rainbows shimmered in the clouds. Entranced, my husband and I sat out on the new porch, sipping drinks. Miraculously, the rare dove had returned to her nest, all past crimes against her kind forgiven. I sat beside my husband, though I knew what losses she was mourning.

EMU AND
ELEPHANT

My brother is the sort of person who plans *outings*. He likes to surround himself with people, his children, his girlfriends, even his sister, and *do* things. Which is how I find myself at the zoo on a spring evening with three of his children and one of his girlfriends. The children come from three different marriages, and the girlfriends get thinner every year. This one is tan and blond, a *golfer*, who my brother swears is not anorexic.

We've arrived an hour early for a "Concert at the Zoo," and after my brother and his girlfriend have spread a blanket and arranged take-out food and paper plates, the two younger children run off to play on the grass. My nephew, who is now six-foot-two and taller than his father, and I wander down the road to look at the animals.

It doesn't matter to my brother whom we are seeing in the concert—it's the idea of the outing that counts—but the act happens to be Chuck Berry. My nephew, who has two guitars I know of, admits to me, "I'm not sure who he is."

I raise an eyebrow. "Long Distance Information? Memphis, Tennessee?"

"Oh him," my nephew says.

We walk over to a large compound surrounded by chainlink where, separated from us by a largely *unnecessary* moat, several long-legged birds with dirt-colored fur huddle near the back. The sign tells us these are emus. Though I have to admit they aren't very interesting, my nephew is not looking at them at all. He is riveted by the people arriving for the concert. They clearly do not live in the upscale suburbs he does. Their attire runs to tank tops and T-shirts, and their bodies are either ropy and tattooed, or excessively round. My brother saunters up as if he's *mingling* with his guests, and my nephew says under his breath, angling for a laugh,

"I've never seen so many people who are calorically challenged."

I say loudly, "You mean FAT?"

My brother shies away from me, his palm held up. "I didn't say it. I didn't say it. You said it."

All the time I was growing up, my brother teased me ruthlessly about my weight, which I realize only now, in my mid-forties, was *normal*. Though a little on the sturdy side, I've always landed safely in the middle of the height-to-weight chart. But because of my brother, I spent nearly half my life ashamed in front of grocery clerks. In college, I used to walk to the corner store to buy a candy bar, convinced the clerk was saying to himself, "*That's* just what she needs." My brother—who is definitely not fat—has been on a fat-free diet for years. I can never find anything to eat at his house. The refrigerator is full of cheese that tastes like bleached and shredded tires.

My brother leaves us in front of the emus, and we can't go any farther into the zoo. An employee wearing khakis and kneesocks stops to chat—I wonder if they still call them *keepers*. I wonder about my brother's girlfriend. Does she call herself a *golfer?* Was *golfing* even listed on career day?

The keeper is explaining that the road into the rest of the zoo is closed because of the elephants. They have to put the elephants away on concert nights. The music, apparently, upsets them. This interests me and my nephew a great deal. We want to know if it's any particular kind of music, and are the inside cages *soundproof?*

I keep thinking of Tarzan movies. As kids, my brother and I went to many, many movies. Sometimes, my mother dropped us off downtown—we must have been only nine and eleven—and, without telling her, we went to separate shows in different grand and ornate movie palaces. But we both know all about things almost forgotten, like pygmy blowguns and the secret burial ground of the elephants.

I tell my nephew, "The elephants can't come out because they're FAT." He winces, covering both ears.

When it finally rolls around, the concert itself isn't bad. Chuck Berry even does his famous, low guitar walk across the stage, though he looks ancient. His glistening skin tents across his nose and cheekbones. My brother leans over to me and says, "I thought he was dead."

"Might be," I reply.

We laugh so hard I remember why I go on these damn outings with my brother. He has devised a kind of system whereby—though he would rather be dead than fat, and rather be fat than related to someone who is—I am different. After all these years, he's issued me a special dispensation. Somewhere, deep inside, I think he worries he might find himself alone someday, with only me, the sturdy one, to help him find his way back through the trees.

FOX

Henry never has much to say, so I begin to describe to him what I see out the window. We're speaking on the phone, long-distance, and I gaze far out into the field where the hay crew has dropped a single bale. Behind it, I see the young foxes. They look like blurred, buff-colored shapes against the grass, but I can make out one with his paws propped up on the hay bale trying to survey the field. I count one, two, three kits—six tall, pointed ears.

At the other end of the field, a pair of sandhill cranes saunters slowly in the direction of the hay bale.

"The foxes are planning an ambush," I tell Henry.

I give him a play-by-play account of the action, the cranes on their stilt-like legs grazing their way down the field, and the foxes popping up and down behind the hay like cartoon soldiers peeking out of—foxholes. The cranes are six times their size.

"The little guys," I say to Henry, "have delusions of grandeur."

One of the cranes calls, and I step out on the porch and extend the phone away from me. The sound is prehistoric, a dry, wooden rachet slowly cranking. In the spring and fall, migrating cranes fly so low over my roof, I can hear the creaking of their wings, the displacement of great *whumps* of air.

"Did you hear it?" I ask Henry.

"No," he says, "I couldn't hear a thing. The couple downstairs are fighting."

As unlikely as it seems, Henry and I met through a newspaper ad, and though I live in Idaho and he in Denver, we've been carrying on this phone romance for several months now. His voice on the phone is deep and warm, naturally seductive, and I believe he must be wonderful with patients. As we're talking, he is paged by the hospital. Henry is the psychologist who responds when someone drunk or crazy shows up in Emergency. I sit down on the steps and we continue talking while he changes clothes, telling me, "I'm walking to the closet. Looking for a pair of jeans. Now I'm looking for a shirt." He puts the phone down while he draws the T-shirt he's wearing over his head and pulls on a clean one.

I picture him in my mind, the all-American boy in his white T-shirt, jeans, and sneakers, but in fact, he's almost forty and looks a little like Abraham Lincoln. This belies the sound of his voice, which tonight is boyish and amused.

I tell him the cranes are drawing near the foxes, but they don't see the trap. I explain how foxes are born every spring in a den underneath my barn. Every year I wait to see how many, and this year I've counted five in all. As soon as the mother departs in the evening to hunt, they begin to pop in and out of gaps in the barn like puppets in a Punch and Judy show. Later, I see the mother returning by indirect routes, large rodents dangling in her jaws.

My ex-husband once found a kit with a length of orange baling twine twisted around its neck. He snagged the end of the string with a long pole and reeled the fighting kit in close enough to free it. "You wouldn't believe what a knot of muscle that little thing was," he told me. "Like a kitten from Hell."

When he later took a job off the ranch, it fell to me to watch the heifers, young cows heavy with first calves. I set the alarm and, three times during the night, bundled up and made my way by flashlight out into the dark. Generally, all the cows had bedded down in a circle near the barn, and I slowly walked around each one, my heavy boots buoyed by rafts of frozen straw and manure. I played the light on one cow, then another, listening for strained and labored breathing.

One morning, just after midnight, I heard a scream in the distance, a shriek so terrible, it froze me in place. When it came again, I couldn't tell if it was animal or human—or something else. I edged closer to the cows, as if they could protect me. The night was vast and black, with icy, pinprick stars. The cows went on with their heavy sighing, their breath steaming in my light, and it wasn't until the following spring, when I actually saw a fox stand on a rise in the field and scream at the dogs that I realized what kind of animal could bark like that.

Henry has to hang up and drive to the emergency room. I've asked him what it's like there, but he never has too much to say. Partly, what he sees is confidential. But partly, Henry doesn't know what to say. He laughs sometimes when a drunk has kept him and a shift of nurses running all night long. But when I ask him how he feels about a girl who had her stomach pumped, he doesn't answer me.

Some weeks ago, I picked Henry up at the airport and drove him here. He hardly spoke a single word on the entire ride, a trip of sixty miles. We were both afraid of disappointment. I was afraid I would look too old—that I would not be who he imagined. The visit was miserable for both of us, but the next week I flew to Denver as we had planned. He had a tidy apartment with two bedrooms and a view, but I couldn't imagine what he did with his time in there. After I flew home, we went back to talking almost daily on the phone. I think each of us suspected we would never meet again, and yet we kept on calling.

. . .

I sit on the steps, picturing Henry driving through the city toward the next young girl who is trapped between longing and shame. By now, the kits are excited—the cranes are nearly close enough to rush, but just as the foxes pounce, the cranes unfold their enormous wings, stride into an awkward lift, and glide over the field. In seconds, they are above the barn and flying toward me. They are so close, I can see the fuselages of their bodies, but they are not like planes. They undulate like porpoises or seals. Watch birds closely: wild geese and robins, the smallest of the hummingbirds. They don't so much fly; they swim through the air, like creatures from a great, remembered sea.

GOOSE

It happened in a matter of minutes. My dog jumped the fence and killed three ducks and two geese. I had gone into my studio, a former garage and tool shop, and left the dog outside the door. The instant I heard the honking of the geese, I ran out. The gate into the poultry yard was closed, but the dog was just outside their cage, lunging and barking—in her mind, playing with the geese who had backed into the corner of their room-sized enclosure. I drove her off, screaming at her. I grabbed her by the collar, dragged her to the main house, and locked her in.

Three white ducks lay calmly dead just outside the goose cage. The gray and white goose lay just inside, where he had turned in defense. The white Chinese goose had fallen in the corner, behind an open door into the storage room. While I removed the dead birds, the other eight geese called back and forth in agitation, and when I drove them from the cage, they returned to the door.

Geese don't always mate for life. If one of a pair dies, the other might take a new mate. But our geese mourned. They stood about with their heads low and their feathers drooping, and gave off despondent sounds, low honks that seemed to be emitted at random.

My husband accused me of leaving the gate open, but I know I did not. He blamed me for the dead birds. I reminded him that the dog could easily jump in the window of a full-sized pickup truck. She was fascinated by the geese and ducks and spent hours, every nerve alert, watching them from her side of the fence. What had made us think that she wouldn't go over?

It was spring and the geese had been mating. This was a violent undertaking where the ganders grasped the necks of the geese in their beaks and held them underwater. There was noise and struggling and a beating of great wings. It would have seemed to the dog, I thought, like a wanton game in which she might join. Or perhaps it seemed to her that the geese were in distress. The sound of struggle might have driven her instincts past their limits.

When a dog kills farm poultry, the cure is to tie a dead bird around its neck and make the dog drag it. I knew this method worked, but I couldn't punish the dog for being what she was. When I dragged her away, screaming at her, she had looked bewildered. I had hit her. Now I was sorry. I was sorry for the geese—and sorry for the dog.

Later, my husband told me it was all my fault—for buying the geese in the first place. Because our house came with a large poultry yard and cage, I had wanted geese. As it turned out, to order the geese by mail, I had to buy a minimum of ten. Shipped on the day they are hatched, goslings retain enough nourishment from the egg to make a journey by mail, but they need the warmth of other small bodies.

When the post office called me, I drove to town and picked up the box from Iowa. It was less than a foot square, with ten yellow babies crowded inside. When I held one in my palm, it nodded off to sleep like a little, fluffy drunk.

My husband had accused me of believing I could just send off in the mail and get things to love, yet he suffered more than I did when the geese were killed. He buried the carcasses, but afterward, he avoided the goose yard. The surviving geese gathered just outside my studio, and I watched them in their confusion. Aware of the absence among them—a break in the order of things—they stood about honking in low moans, like lost cattle. But in time, they forgot. They ventured back into their yard and nested in a pile of branches and lawn trimmings. We had raised the fence, but the dog again took up her vigil on the other side, and the geese grew so bold as to graze right up to her and lower their beaks in aggression.

For long periods of time, I have forgotten the day the birds were killed. The world reknit at the seams and went on. A higher order of animal, my husband won't ever forget. Mated for life and unable to grieve, he wants someone to blame.

HEN

At the beginning of each summer, when Gene returned to her house on the western edge of Texas, she let herself think, "I could live here all year round." Gazing into the empty distance, she saw in her mind pink sandstone canyons, great fissures in the flat ground, invisible from passing cars. When she took her run into the country, she knew she was crossing the trails of ancient native tribes and beneath her feet, underground rivers had carved and polished glistening sandstone caves.

She had been home just a week when she carried her tray and coffee onto the porch and surprised a skinny, speckled hen perched on the rail. The hen eyed her, as chickens do, as if *she* were the intruder, and remained vigilant while Gene drank her coffee, pushing herself back and forth on the swing with one foot.

She asked her mother to inquire in town, see if anybody was missing a scrawny speckled hen. If they were, no one admitted it, and in any event, after a day or two, the chicken wandered off.

It always happened that when she first arrived in June, she took the trouble to visit with her relatives, her parents' friends, but after a few weeks, she remained in her house, learning again by heart the pattern on the linoleum, an extravagance of pink and gray begonias.

Alone, she felt "chosen" when the chicken returned to roost on the lid of the wood box, just outside the door. With no straw or grass or nesting box, she settled her feathered breast on the slope of the plywood lid. Gene sat opposite, glancing up from her work from time to time to see the hen nod off.

In the cool of the evening, she slumped in the swing, downing a quart of grapefruit juice, and then too often a bottle of wine. She reported to the chicken what she'd seen on her run—a fat coyote lobbing along a fence line. "Goin' to be an *early* winter," she warned.

On the first of August, her cousin Mack drove into town to meet with her dad regarding one of their construction jobs. Raymond, who had served in the Pacific during World War II, loved Mack and had been inviting him to dinner since he and Gene were childhood friends. He tried to induce Mack to talk about Vietnam, but over the years, her cousin had become adept at turning the conversation back to Raymond, who had endless stories of his shipboard life and liberties in every port.

That afternoon, she skipped her run since she and Mack were both expected for dinner. She showered early and dressed in a clean pair of slacks and a crisp, sleeveless blouse. Sitting on the bed her grandmother had been born in, in the house her grandfather had built, she buckled on stout walking sandals, though she was only driving to the other side of town.

.   .   .

A tall, angular woman, she had to unfold herself from the driver's seat, and she could see Raymond watching from the picture window. She smiled, thinking of him scoffing at the sports car, saying, "What's the practicality of that?"

Mack hadn't come. He'd declined the invitation to finish some roof repairs while his wife and son remained in Carlsbad, and Gene was so surprised by the depth of her disappointment, she didn't notice right away how the atmosphere had changed in her parents' familiar house. The table had been set as if for Sunday dinner, and her father wore a pressed blue shirt and slacks. Her mother moved about the kitchen with an apron over her skirt and pearl-white blouse.

"What's up?" she asked. "We expecting the queen?"

They both smiled at her, proud, yet somehow diffident. "Before dinner," Raymond said, "we want to take care of a little business."

"Does this require a drink?"

"It could." Her father opened a beer for each of them, set hers on the tablecloth, and motioned for her to sit down. Her mother removed her apron and seated herself at one end of the dining table while her father took his place at the other.

Sliding his plate aside, he centered a worn accordion file in front of him.

"We need to tell you what we wish," he said, "if anything should happen to us."

"All right," she thought. Her dad nodded at her mother and slipped official-looking papers from the file. He talked about the plot they had paid taxes on for so many years in the cemetery, about headstones, and finally, about the funeral. When her mother began to list specific hymns, Gene stopped her.

"You planning on going somewhere?"

"Well, no. Not right away."

"Good. I don't want to know all this right now."

"We've written it all down," her mother said. "So you will know. You'll be glad for it when the time comes."

She tried to joke with them. "Only the good die young."

She helped her mother serve pot roast and peas and potatoes, and it wasn't until after dessert and coffee that her dad brought up the real business he'd had in mind.

"Of course," her dad said, "you'll be the one to inherit."

"I don't need to hear about that either," she said.

"Well, there might be some little trouble."

"Why?"

"Well," her mother said, watching Gene carefully. She stopped, her pale-blue eyes filled with care and embarrassment. "We adopted you."

Gene saw the tears in her eyes, and felt her own throat contract and her face suffuse with heat. She was too stunned to speak. The silence in the room seemed permanent, a vast sheet of plate glass between them.

"Why didn't you tell me before?" she asked. "I'm forty-five years old."

"It just never came up," her dad began, but her mother interrupted.

"No," she said, "I just didn't want you to know. I didn't want you to think we didn't love you."

"You were ashamed," Gene said. She saw it in her mother's eyes.

"Not of you," she said. "I was ashamed of holding such a lie. I was terrified some other person would tell you."

"Other people knew?" she asked, her voice finally cracking.

"We didn't tell them." It was her dad who answered. "When we brought you back with us from San Diego, they just knew."

"How old was I?"

"A baby," her mother said. "Just a baby."

"How? How could anybody know?"

"You can't hide a thing like that in this town," her dad said. "Stop and think about it."

She found herself pushing her chair back from the table.

"I guess I will," she said.

Her mother looked pale and anguished. Her dad folded both hands into one fist and rested them on the table.

Gene stepped out into the summer evening and began to walk in no particular direction. A runner and an athlete, this is what she had always done—found a place inside her own body that moved in a familiar way, and thought of nothing but the steady rhythm of her heart and breath. But it didn't work this time. Crowds of imaginary people invaded her thoughts. All these years while she had felt at home, others knew she was a rank imposter. She could feel the slap of their disdain—their kindness and superiority.

Afraid to drive the car, she walked the few blocks to Mack and Mary's house. At the back door, she hesitated. It was a door as familiar as her own, one she'd walked through without knocking for so many years. The kitchen was dark, but she could hear voices on the television. She knocked on the screen door. When no one came, she opened the door and called, "Mack? Mack, are you in there?"

When Mack flipped on the light and appeared in his jeans and stocking feet, she couldn't keep back tears.

"What? What is it?"

Gene stumbled into the kitchen and, unable to look at him, butted her head into his shoulder, wrapping her arms around his chest.

"What is it? You hurt? Let me see." Mack tried to push her away, to hold her at arm's length, but she held on.

"Not hurt," she said.

He walked her into the sitting room and they sank onto the couch. The voices from the television went on talking. She couldn't remember ever crying so hard. She felt as if her body were twisting inside out, every secret she'd ever had displayed for anyone to see. She gasped for air.

Mack held her close and patted her back as if she were a fretful baby. He smoothed her hair and skimmed tears from her face with the edge of his palm. They rocked and he said nothing more.

"Where's Mary?" she asked him.

"Carlsbad, Teddy, remember?"

"With Ted," she repeated.

When she was able to stop the tears, she told Mack everything her parents had said. He hadn't known. His folks might, he thought. He'd have to think about it, but he understood the meaning of her news.

She let Mack hold her, as she never would have in all the years they had been friends. She lifted her face and kissed him on the mouth.

Very gently, Mack took her shoulders and pushed her away.

She walked back to her car and drove herself home. Her house, the steps, the porch looked ghostly. The screen door creaked when she touched it, and an explosion went off to her right—a parachute snapped open, an umbrella blowing inside out. Her heart seemed to stop in her chest before she saw the chicken, all feathers and scrawny feet, puffed up in alarm.

"Shush," she said. "You're not takin' any harm."

She'd had a professor once tell her, "Never be ashamed of what a fool you make of yourself for love. You've got millions of years of biology pushing you to do just that." But in the morning she felt naked and exposed in her own house, as if any person passing on the road could see her, though the shades were drawn. She pulled a windbreaker over her nightgown and set up a tray, but after she buttered a piece of toast and poured her coffee, she hesitated. "You're a fool," she thought, "and everybody knows it."

Eventually she carried her coffee outside and sat back on the faded cushions of the swing. The speckled hen swivelled her head and stared. Gene pictured herself walking down to the store with the chicken following behind her on a string.

"There's those two old maids," she said.

She thought of Mack standing in the kitchen in his socks. Surges of fear, like tiny shocks, touched her and she leaned into them, trying to locate the pleasure in the pain, until she finally admitted to herself that she was waiting for him. A sense of desolation overtook her. Mack would not be coming.

In the afternoon, her father woke her by knocking the back of his big fist against the screen door, bouncing the door in its frame.

"Hold on," she said, "I'm coming," and reached the door in time to see him flush the squawking chicken off the porch.

"Don't let that chicken roost there," he said. "Chickens have diseases."

"Hey Raymond," she said.

"Got any coffee?"

"Sure."

She turned back to the kitchen to reheat the coffee, but she could hear the floorboards creaking underneath his shifting weight. When she handed him the china cup, he held it by the rim and set it on the table. In one motion, he drew a chair under himself and sat down, bending to blow on the surface of his coffee. A lank of hair had fallen over his forehead, and a tiny bead of sweat rolled down his temple.

"Eugenia," he said. "Your mother and I . . . Your mother asked me to come."

He faltered, but she didn't speak.

"You're going to have to forgive us," he said. "We never meant you any harm. I think—" He raised his hand and sucked in breath. "We thought you *were* our girl."

She tilted her head back to keep the tears from coming.

"We forgot you weren't."

Gene stared at the fragile cup resting by his callused hand. It was not her grandmother's cup.

"Come down to the place, come see your mother," Raymond said.

"I'll try," she said. "Maybe I'll come later on."

After he was gone, Gene remained sitting at the table. Her parents had always been so proud of their daughter the professor. She had not told them her department was closing—no oil, no geology. In the winter, she longed for her house on the high, empty plains, but suddenly she had to resist the urge to throw her clothes in the car and go.

When the heat of the day began to lift, she changed into her shorts and ran toward the foothills on game trails that she knew crossed ancient hunting routes. She pushed herself until sweat flew from her hair when she stopped to shake it from her eyes. As she turned back toward town, she felt as if only her heels and toes touched the earth, that she herself might fly off any moment.

As she slowed to cool down, she saw Mack sitting on the top step of her porch, his long legs reaching to the ground, his hat tipped over his eyes.

"You got company," he said, nodding at the chicken.

"So I see."

He lifted a bottle of beer from a brown sack beside him and nodded. "Get cleaned up," he said. "I'll take you for a ride."

They lay side by side in the grass beside the river, their faces open to the sky, to so many stars Gene felt them shift and jolt, as if entire constellations might lurch and fall behind the far edge of the earth. She flattened herself to the ground, spinning in a centrifuge, a carnival ride where the floor drops out below.

Mack counted for her seven shooting stars, comet tails of molten light so quick they seemed to vanish just as they appeared.

"Why didn't you marry me when I asked you?" Mack said.

"You never did."

"Yeah, I did. Right when I got discharged."

She shifted onto her elbow and stared at his profile.

"I thought you were my cousin," she said.

"No," he said. "That wasn't it."

They parked Mack's truck in his own driveway and walked back to her solitary house. The hen shifted and clucked when Mack opened the door. She knew he would stay through the night, and she let every touch reach deep into her bones, to the girl she had been and the woman she was now. Slowly edging down the sheet, Mack kissed the tender skin along the curve of her hip. He looked up to see her face. Never had making love been, in every touch and moment, about love, as if behind each one of his kisses, there was a reservoir of strength refilling from within.

Before daylight, they dressed and sat down on the edge of the bed. Gene understood now that every man she'd ever been with had disappointed her—because he wasn't Mack. She looked at him and brushed the tips of her fingers along his cheekbone. His hair had turned gray at the temples, and the sharp jawline she loved was beginning to soften and round.

"What are we going to do now?" she asked him.

He wrapped an arm around her shoulders and pulled her against him before he said, "Not a thing."

They drank coffee from the painted china cups and afterward, she followed Mack out on the porch, expecting the hen to protest. But the speckled bird wasn't there. Gene saw a dark spot on the lid of the wood box and reached for it as she would for a coin dropped on the floor. A dark red smudge came off on her fingertips.

In the weeds beside the porch they found a scattering of feathers, and a few steps beyond, the hen, her neck twisted back over her wing like the head of a sleeping swan. Gene looked at Mack for explanation.

"I've seen skunks do like that," he said. "It could have been a skunk."

They buried the hen behind the house, under a twisted, gray apple tree. Gene firmed the earth with her palm and stood.

"Look," Mack whispered.

When she turned to look, his shoulder touched hers, and it was as if the warmth of his body passed through her skin, from cell to cell, and again, deep into her bones. On the eastern horizon, the sun lifted from a pool of smoky clouds and struck the narrow windows of her house. They sheeted gold and winked. From the distant foothills, they must have looked like tiny mirrors flashing code, Gene thought—an urgent message, or a sign of life.

IMPALA

My husband is a terrible driver, not the worst I've seen, but dangerous. He watches the scenery instead of the road, and he's the only driver I know who, sober, seems to have serious trouble driving inside the lines. I will be talking to him, and suddenly, I feel the rough bump of the asphalt shoulder, the jerk and swerve as he corrects the wheel and pulls back into his lane.

He, naturally, denies that there is anything wrong with his driving, but I come from a long line of bad drivers—so I know. I remember particularly a drive in

California with my mother, who, having had a few drinks, took a winding road up through a canyon to visit my aunt and uncle. Even as children, my sister and I were not *quiet*. In fear of our lives, we begged my mother to slow down and stay in one lane.

I still ride with my husband, because car trips are our happiest times. We are driving across the desert in New Mexico, heading for Carlsbad Caverns. He has been telling me that north of where we are, near the White Sands Missile Range, there are feral emus. *Feral emus?* I have a hard time picturing this, and I am skeptical. He says he has it on good authority that, years ago, emus were imported and released for sport hunting, that some escaped and have become wild.

When he bumps just slightly off the road, I sit rigid.

"Relax," he tells me.

"I can't," I say, and tell him how, while my mother worked, my grandmother picked us up from school for appointments at the doctor or the dentist, and drove us from Glendale to Burbank, avoiding the freeway. We lived on a long, narrow street where cars parked bumper-to-bumper on both sides, and on the way home, my sister and I cringed. When we could, we called out like river guides, helping my grandmother navigate between the looming doors and fenders. We learned to be vigilant.

It was my mother, though, who drove us out to vast, empty parking lots and taught us to drive in her tiny red Studebaker Lark—with a stick shift. She kept up a singsong litany that we can imitate to this day: "A little bit of gas . . . and a little bit of clutch . . . a little bit of gas . . . AND a little bit of clutch . . . BRAKE BRAKE BRAKE!" My grandmother had bought the car for my mother that we might make the trip from Florida, where my father had deserted us, back to California in safety. We didn't mind the car—we loved the "new car" smell—but we also understood that it was the cheapest car on the market. We knew because my grandmother, despite her stocks and bonds, was cheap.

My sister and I both learned to drive, but we were terrified of backing out of our driveway, where stucco walls loomed close on either side. This was just possible with the Lark—but one day my mother drove home from the school where she taught in a brand-new Chevrolet.

This was around the time that John F. Kennedy was president, and cars, up until then, had had unique designs. Each year, my sister and I watched for the new models, and we could have told you in an instant the make of any car. But this car was one of the first with no fins, no portholes, no distinctive grille. It was a huge, generic car. A Chevy Impala.

Our lives were instantly improved and complicated; the car was a dream to drive—if you could get it out of the driveway and down the road. We lived in dread of hitting something, but on the freeways, it cruised like a huge parade float, making us the commanders of all we surveyed.

My husband looks at me, a thought forming on his face.

"Watch the road," I say.

He turns back to the road, which stretches straight across the desert, as far as you can see. There is not another single car in sight.

"It wasn't *emus*," he says. "It was ibex."

"*Walter*," I say. "An emu is a *bird*. An *ibex* is an antelope."

"Antelope," he says. "I *meant* an antelope."

My mother, who set great store by such things, was dismayed that my first boyfriend drove a Volkswagen. She invited him out to dinner—then insisted that he drive *her* car. I was embarrassed and sat in the back, but Bruce was older than I, a safe, methodical driver, who, unbelievably, was amused by my mother. He settled into the driver's seat, adjusted the mirrors and familiarized himself with the controls. Out on the street, he turned and informed my mother, "I'm only driving my half of the car. You're on your own."

Eventually, my grandmother stuck mostly to driving herself back and forth to the market. She accomplished this early in the morning, before the roads were crowded. The day came, of course, when I was riding with her, driving along our narrow street toward home, when she hit a car parked at the curb. I heard the metal-on-metal scrape, that awful sound. But my grandmother heard nothing. When we arrived at the house, I had to convince her to let me jog back and leave her phone number—but she hadn't felt a thing. She didn't know she'd sideswiped a car.

When my grandmother died, she had a new, metallic-green Ford parked in her garage—purchased without one single "extra"—no air-conditioning, no clock, no radio—and my mother had bought a new Mercedes. By then, however, my sister and I did the driving.

My husband pulls safely into the parking lot of the Holiday Inn in Carlsbad, and we both gaze in wonder at the desert landscaping, the spiked ocotillo blooming flame red against the stucco walls. He comes around the car to open the door and help me into my chair. Though I can do it easily myself, he wheels me to the door and opens it.

Inside the air-conditioned room he says, "It wasn't ibex . . . I think it was an African antelope. The one with the black and white face. What is that?"

I shake my head. I don't know.

It isn't until the trip is over and we are back in California, in our house in the hills, that I pull out the dictionary: *Webster's New World Dictionary of the American Language*, College Edition, copyright 1965. This is the book my grandmother presented to me when I went away to college. In it, I find ibex, "Any of several varieties of wild goat of Europe, Asia, or Africa," and oryx, "Any of a group of large African antelope with long, straight horns projecting backwards." It is the oryx that has the black and white face and it is the oryx that, in fact, runs wild near White Sands National Monument. But nowhere, under any spelling, not even in the *Oxford English Dictionary* (abridged, I admit) do I find the word impala.

I haul out all the dictionaries—paging through them one by one. It isn't until a 1967 edition, printed in 1979, that I find impala, a *Zulu* word—introduced into our language, as far as I can tell, by *Detroit*. I wheel myself out to the garage to find Walter rummaging for bolts. He's taken it on himself to install bars on all the windows facing the canyon and dry hills. I wait for him to stop what he is doing.

"They had wild antelope in L.A. when I was a girl," I say. "They appeared about the time I was in high school—and ran free all around here . . . " I twirl my hand in the air. ". . . with the Mustangs."

JOSIE

My father named all his dogs "Josie." After my parents divorced, it was the only thing my mother kept in active play: We named our dog Josie, too. She was a black mongrel dog, part collie, I imagine, and part cocker spaniel. I have a photograph of myself sitting on the hood of a car, with a cluster of small puppies displayed on a towel before me. I must be eight or nine. My feet are bare, and I'm wearing shorts and a kid's striped T-shirt. I am smiling.

This is a rare photograph. I have dozens of me standing solemnly beside my brother and sister, my arms beside my skirt, my large hands hanging down like plumb bobs. But in this picture, I am happy.

There had been a day, a year or two before, when my best friend whispered to me that she knew someone with puppies to give away. The two of us scrambled through the back alleys of our apartment complex, visited the puppies, then found a place between two high, wooden fences, where we became coconspirators.

Positive our mothers would never let us bring home puppies, we worked all morning planning how to keep the puppy hidden, how each night, one of us would sneak out with food. We scoured the garbage cans behind the buildings and returned with a cardboard box. To keep the puppy in the wedge where the fences met, we arranged a line of crossing sticks.

At dusk, we went home to ask our mothers the question we knew would be answered with "No." My mother stood in the kitchen heating TV dinners. I pulled out the chrome and plastic dinette chair and propped one knee on the seat, teetering back and forth, and explained the situation.

"So," I concluded, "could we have a puppy?"

"All right," my mother said.

I couldn't believe it. After dinner, we walked together, my brother, my sister, my mother, and I, and picked out a puppy—black, because my father's dogs had always been black. And we named her Josie. I was sad to give up the plan I'd made with my friend and in a way, to lose the friend, herself. Her mother had told her "No."

We lived in an apartment in air force housing on a peninsula that reached down into Tampa Bay. From my window, I could see across patchy Bermuda grass to the road and beyond it to the shore, where the polluted water was posted off-limits. But the rain came in off the Gulf nearly every afternoon that time of year.

My sister and I shared a room where we slept on metal army cots. My brother slept on the foldout couch in the living room. The clearest memory I have of that time—one of the clearest and best memories I have—is of lying on my cot with the window open. I have the puppy circled in my arm, and Florida rain is cooling us, splashing against the window screen as we fall asleep.

In those days, people didn't buy dog food—dogs ate table

scraps. I'm surprised there were enough in our family to feed a good-sized dog, but Josie grew up to be the kind of matronly black dog that most children have. When we were forced by a change of regulations to move off the base, she went with us to the huge, old wooden house my mother rented, a house with a silver tin roof on a brick-cobbled street named Jules Verne Court.

After two years in that house, word came down, as it does to children—mysteriously—that we were moving across the country. My mother sold all the furniture except a few things she and my father had bought when he was stationed in what she called "the Orient," and she produced a military foot-locker for each of us. We were told we could take only as many clothes and toys as would fit in the locker.

I remember the trip—all of us sunburned and freezing in the air-conditioned motel rooms. The Mississippi River. The Grand Canyon. Fighting in the backseat until my mother turned around and slapped us. I remember how excited we were to arrive at my grandmother's house, but I don't remember missing Josie.

.   .   .

Josie had one litter of puppies before my mother had her spayed. I know, because I have the photograph. In the black and white snapshot, the pups are still too small to give away, no more than three weeks old, the shape of rising loaves you might hold in one hand. But I had held each one so often and so closely that I could tell them apart by smell.

Around that time, my mother had a mysterious boyfriend—a man in starched khakis, with sandy hair and wire-rimmed glasses. I remember that he was a master sergeant and that later I found papers in my mother's closet naming her as "corespondent" in his divorce. Though by the time I discovered the papers, I hadn't seen him in a while.

When the puppies were small, he asked me, "How can you tell the boy puppies from the girls?"

I answered in perfect seriousness—I could tell by the smell. When he laughed—and my mother joined him—I wasn't embarrassed, because I didn't understand the joke until much later. I knew the obvious differences between male and female puppies. I was giving him the inside scoop.

My mother was so beautiful then. She had long, perfect legs and wore her hair the way she'd worn it in the forties, though this was 1959. She was only thirty-eight years old. I was eleven, going on twelve, and up until then, I loved her without question. When she was away from the house, I longed for her return. Though like most parents of her time, she seldom spoke to us at all except to scold, there was a day when a terror suddenly overtook me, a fear that my mother would someday die. I cried, inconsolable, and for a few minutes, my mother sat on the couch and held me on her lap, rocking me and saying, "No no no. I'm not going to die."

Though my mother never said so, I knew she hadn't even tried to give Josie away. She had had her put to sleep. She must have lied about it at the time or we would have cried and protested. But somehow, I knew. I have always known, because my mother could be ruthless in her practicality. Faced with driving three children and towing a trailer across the country by herself, she wouldn't take a dog.

I was nearly a teenager, going into the eighth grade. I wanted to learn how to dance, and wear my hair in a French twist. I longed to leave my awkward self behind and move across the country. The trip didn't change my life as I had hoped. Instead, as we became teenagers, my mother became a tired household policeman, and I don't remember ever loving her again in that simple way I had.

My mother died more than ten years ago, yet even now, I dream she is alive. The dreams are so vivid, so convincing, I feel a great reprieve—until I wake up, stunned by my mistake and mired in sorrow. Maybe I accepted what my mother did when she left Josie behind, because I should have known better than to ask for a dog. Maybe I'd been waiting, all that time, to pay for my mistake. My friend and I had been right to think we needed secrecy. When my mother said, "All right, you can have a puppy," I should have asked her, "For how long?"

KESTREL

A kestrel is the smallest North American falcon, a copper-colored bird the size of a man's hand. On the way to town, I collided with one. It seemed to dive in from the sky and crash into the hood of my car. I was so stunned, I pulled over to the shoulder of the road, my heart pounding. I couldn't believe the bird had hit me, that it hadn't sheered away at the last moment as birds always do. It was late morning in early summer and no other cars were coming. I walked back to where the falcon lay in the center of the road. Its eyes were closed, but I could see the speckled breast heave.

I scooped it up and placed it in a box in the back of my station wagon and drove into town. I had no idea what to do for an injured hawk, but I thought, "I'll find a telephone and call the veterinarian." On Main Street, I left the box in the car, ran into the antique shop, and tried to explain to my friend Jean what had happened. I phoned the vet clinic and spoke to the receptionist. "Call Birdman," she said and dictated a number. I called, but all I could do was leave a message.

I felt terrible. Jean followed me out to the car and stared into the box. She looked at me inquiringly through the thick, distorting lenses of her glasses. She was from New York, a timid woman who—though a newcomer—was liked for her intelligence and calm.

"I didn't hit it," I told her. "It hit *me*." I had such a strong sense of emergency, like caffeine in my veins, telling me to do something. I wanted so badly to save the falcon—but Jean seemed a little mystified by my concern. Perhaps she thought, "It's just a bird." It wasn't "just a bird" to me.

As a girl, I loved falconry. I have no idea where this passion came from, but I pored through books and knew that all falconers began with the smallest of the wild hawks, the sparrow hawk, which, in my girl's heart, was more marvelous because it was a great hawk in miniature. I dreamed of how I would house the hawks and wear them on my arm, how I would have fringed leather gauntlets and feathered hoods for every bird.

In my real child's life, I tried to save every sick or injured mockingbird that fell within our yard. I gathered babies fallen from their nests and kept them in boxes in my room, waking in the night to feed them a mash of milk and bread through eyedroppers. I agonized when I couldn't stay home from school to nurse them. I never enlisted the help of an adult. I never saved a single bird.

As Jean and I watched, the kestrel shook itself awake. It stood, but didn't try to move or fly. I thought, "Oh thank God, it's only stunned." I left Jean and drove home, trying to think what I could use for a cage. When I got back to the ranch, I hauled a large dog crate—an airplane carrier—from the shed and set it up on the mud porch, a small room off the kitchen with windows all around.

I kept phoning and finally, I reached Birdman and explained the situation. He said, "Feed it worms. I'll be out to look at it as soon as I can get there." I had heard of Birdman before, though I'd never met him. He was a regular person who had made wild birds his avocation, his expertise growing until his help was sought by everybody in the valley: ranchers, and vets, even Fish and Wildlife agents.

By the time he arrived, the kestrel had perched on a knot of driftwood I'd placed in its cage, swiveling its head to look around and picking at the worms I'd gathered from the garden. Birdman closed the door to the mudroom and reached in the cage with his bare hand.

"Hey there," he said.

The bird screamed, and its talon sliced a long cut that slowly bloomed with tiny red beads along his arm, but Birdman went on talking.

"Let's just see what's going on here."

He turned the bird over as if it were the tamest parakeet.

"No broken bones, no blood. Looks okay to me," he said.

The kestrel stared daggers at him, fierce in a way only raptors are fierce.

"All I see is a slight injury to the eye," he told me.

He placed the ruffled bird back on its perch and dug in his pocket for a tube of ointment.

"Put this in twice a day," he said.

"Oh sure," I thought. "Me and who else," but I didn't say a thing. Birdman stood up in the small room off my kitchen. I invited him in, but he showed no inclination to follow me into the kitchen. We stood there in close quarters, Birdman still examining the bird with his eyes.

"It could be," he said, "that the eye was injured when she hit your car. Or, it could be that she hit your car because the eye was injured. But this should do the trick.

"What you have to remember," he said, "is just exactly where you picked her up. If she recovers, release her back in that same place."

"It's a she?" I asked.

"Yes," he told me. "She'll have a nest this time of year— but you don't need to worry. The male bird will keep the babies fed. What you need to do is catch her mice. I can bring you some tomorrow. I've got some in my freezer. But if you could trap some fresh mice, that would be best."

He left instructions for me to call if I needed more help, climbed into his truck, and was gone.

"Mice," I thought. "Certainly have enough of those." I rummaged in the pantry for traps. All farm and ranch houses have plenty of mice, but not so many in the summer. They get to be a problem in the fall and winter, when they come in from the cold. After I set the traps I had, I called my neighbor, who offered to have his grandsons set traps in his granary.

The next morning, a troop of small boys appeared on bicycles. One of them carried a jar of mice—a mother and all of her tiny, pink babies. Unlike Jean, the boys were as awed by the kestrel as I was. They stood in the doorway and gazed at it with great respect, asking me questions. They, too, were anxious that the hawk should live.

I fed the bird once a day and waited for it to spit up bones and fur. I watched it grow stronger and take an interest in the world outside the windows. If I had to handle it, I wore heavy gloves and a padded jacket, and at the beginning, the bird was so fierce and indifferent, I never thought of her as female, but after a few days, the hawk showed so little fear, I was able to let her perch free in the mudroom, spending most of her time on top of the dog carrier. The bird was so lovely, with rusty feathers and black markings so distinct, I found myself watching through the kitchen window for hours on end. I began to harbor a secret desire to keep her.

Birdman had said to feed her for ten days or so, two weeks at the most. When he stopped by again, he wore a heavy leather glove and examined the bird from every angle.

"Looks good," he said. "I think you can try to let her go."

I didn't want to let her go. I kept putting off the day, waiting until a friend could go with me. Finally, I drove alone to the exact spot on the way to town where I had hit the kestrel. Cars and trucks, fast-moving traffic, passed me on the highway, and I pulled off on a dirt road to the side. I had brought the bird in a small box. I carried the container out into the grass at the side of the road, opened it, and let the bird perch on my gloved hand. When I lifted my arm, the bird sat still, alert, scouting out the field of hay before us. Quickly, I threw the bird up and off my hand. She flew due east, straight away from me over the field, and just as she came parallel to the place where I had picked her up, she arced to the left and flew directly north, on the exact path she had been on when I hit her.

People are always asking me why I live on this ranch, alone, in the middle of nowhere. Do I raise horses or ski or run rivers? How do I stand the isolation? As winter is coming and I struggle to get in wood and insulate, my brother calls from his office on Wall Street. He wants to know, "What are you doing there?"

"It takes so long to learn things," I say. I remind him of how I tried to save the birds when I was young, and how time after time I found them cold and lifeless in the morning. I don't know how to tell him I no longer want to have a falcon, but I did, I had one for a little while.

"Worms," I tell him. "When your children bring you baby birds to save—you feed them worms."

LARK

It seemed she heard the song of meadowlarks only as she drove along the back roads in the summer when the hay grew tall in the fields and, in the hot sun, smelled of blooming clover. The sound grew louder as it dropped behind, the way the whistle of a freight train swells and cries, just as you pass it by. The larks flashed above the fence wires, brilliant streaks of yellow. Black-striped breasts. But the song, so much more liquid and lovely than any other birdsong, hovered long after.

As a child, she sometimes took apart lilies and hollyhocks, peeling the flowers down to their sticky, pale centers. A field of clover in the summer heat smells like that pure nectar. The smell drifts on the lightest breeze, coming and going, like subtle shifts in temperature.

But it was December, on the shortest day of the year, when she agreed to house the visiting writer for one night. She was newly alone in the house, newly divorced. It didn't occur to her that this fact alone might make him nervous— she thought she was too old for that. In one of the attic rooms, she prepared a bed with clean sheets, carefully attending to his comfort.

When he arrived, a weathered, handsome man who seemed to know it all too well, they sat by the fire and drank tea. He had already eaten he told her, and no, he'd brought a sleeping bag, he had no need of clean sheets. He inquired about her life—her husband who was gone.

When she finished her short story, he said, "I see it all the time. Couples move to the west because they think they'll have a more 'authentic life.' But they don't make it through one winter. Can't take the cabin fever."

She looked at him, puzzled by the anger and derision in his voice. He was a man in his forties—the published writer of many books on travel and wildlife. A native of the west, he'd flown all over the world writing articles for glossy magazines. It was hard to hear her life reduced to cabin fever.

When she and Bob moved to the ranch, the neighbors hadn't held out much hope for her—the city girl. She could all but hear the women gossiping behind her back. When she painted the kitchen yellow to combat the darkness of the old rooms—built when windows were expensive and electricity was hooked up in the barn before the house— her neighbor said, "Oh, you'll get tired of it, and then you won't be able to paint it over. That yellow will always show right through."

Bob's uncle had scoffed out loud at her attempts to grow a garden. He stood in the yard and stared at her delphiniums, tall blue spikes the color of the sky. "Larkspur," he announced. "I know what that is. Poison to a cow."

He made pronouncements. "Why would a person go to all the trouble to grow a damn tomato when you can buy one at the store?"

But she had surprised them. She had lasted, and it was Bob who had finally gone. He had moved to the city and left her the house. He walked out at Thanksgiving and never came back.

"The winters," she said to the visiting writer, "are not the hard part," though they were hard. She heated the old house with wood that had to be hauled and chopped. Snow drifted up over the first-story windows and had to be shoveled. The cold when she woke in the morning, before the fire in the stove was hot, was an assault that made her muscles cling hard to her bones.

But in the summer, they had been happy. They had gone fishing for trout in the back country, and on the river almost in their own backyard. They had taken driving trips from one end of the Rocky Mountains to the other.

"There were so many things I didn't know," she told the writer. "I didn't know I wouldn't see any birds in the winter. Only ravens and magpies. One year we had an eagle down on the river. But I didn't know that there are places in the world too cold for birds.

"I didn't know you can go out to feed cattle and fall in snow so deep, you can't move. You can't gain a purchase to push yourself back up on the track.

"I didn't know how good it feels when spring comes. How people are like animals. They can sense it in their blood. They wait, and when the air warms up, they want to get out, to twitch and gambol like the calves . . ."

The summers were harder because they were so full, and so short. She and Bob cut their first hay crop on July 4, their second in August. What grew in this high valley grew so well, so luxuriantly, and then it stopped. In August, they had their first killing frost. In September, it could snow. The shortness of it made them feel so old—as if their lives were passing in too great a rush.

The writer informed her, "I've just come from Bali," and began to denounce the impact of tourism. Not a clean industry at all, he told her, but the cause of overcrowding and pollution.

"Did you know," she said, "today is the shortest day of the year? Tomorrow, the day will be longer."

"The rain forest . . ." he began, his voice tense with warning, but she held up her palm.

"It's the only time, after we're grown, when we want the days to go faster."

Although the temperature could fall to forty below in January, she explained, after this day, winter was all down-hill, the hardest part over. When he pushed back in his chair, his handsome face pinched, she described how the cows could sense the early days of spring, how they liked to bust out and run up and down the road, their swollen udders swinging. How enormous flocks of wild geese massed near the river and honked all through the night. She thought, "I could tell him why geese fly in formation," or as the sister in Chekov says, "why the cranes fly, why children are born, why there are stars in the sky." Instead, she took in the stiffness of his posture, a discomfort close to fear, and began to explain to him the Doppler effect, as it applies to meadowlarks.

MOOSE

One of the big differences that struck her after they moved onto the ranch was how when the neighbors phoned, they never announced who was calling. The old men and old women all sounded the same, but they expected her to differentiate between their voices— after all, *they* knew who was calling. Which meant she had to wait to talk about the weather and crops and local elections until some clue came up to tell her who was speaking. Each time her nearest neighbor, Earl, called, she waited politely for him to come to the point,

to tell her what he wanted. It was months before she realized
he was only calling to visit. She felt uncommonly honored by
his company.

Earl was seventy at least, tall and wiry and strong. The
week they moved in, she and her husband were standing
with Earl in the yard when she reached down to shift a bale
of straw. Earl stepped in front of her and hoisted it before she
could. "Oh no," she thought, "not another cowboy." But the
following week, she watched him pull the same maneuver on
her husband.

That April, Earl phoned her in the daytime when her
husband was away. "I've seen a bull moose out in the pasture. . . . He's headed up to your place."

"Can I see him from here?" she said, excited.

"Might be."

"Hold on," she said. "I'll go and look."

She hurried around the small house looking intently out
each window. When she saw nothing, she took the time to
find a pair of heavy binoculars. When she still saw only
mountains and green pastures, she went back to the phone.

"I can't see him," she said. "Which way was he going?"

"Look out the north window," he suggested.

Again, she carried the binoculars to the window and scanned the pasture, close and far. Although a moose is brown, she knew that to locate one in the distance, she had to scan the green landscape for a large black shape. Enormous cows and horses swept past in the round, distorting lenses of the binoculars, but she saw no moose. She returned to the phone and lifted the receiver.

"Earl," she said, "I can't find it."

"April Fools'," he said.

She couldn't believe how well he'd gotten her going. Twice, she'd been off the phone looking, for long minutes each time.

"You stinker," she said. "I'm going to get you."

He laughed his low, dry laugh and let her go.

From time to time, Earl turned his old pickup in to her driveway and waited for her to pull on boots and a jacket and come out. She stood at the window of his truck, freezing. Occasionally he eased out of the truck, and they stood—visiting—exposed in the howling wind and snow. She could never persuade him to come in the house.

Earl's stories always started with begats.

"Well, Henry Wilson was the father to George, but he was married to Loretta, and she was a Barkley from over to Chapin . . . " Sometimes the begats went on so long, she lost the point of the whole story. She never knew who the families were, and despite asking many questions, she never learned where Chapin was. Or Bates, or Hinkley, or Squirrel. Squirrel had been a town, but all the others had been Mormon wards, place-names only old-timers used anymore.

After Earl drove on, his truck heavy with stacked hay bales, she might get a call from his wife: "Has Earl been down that way?" Her voice lilted, a western voice with long, southern vowels and neat, clipped consonants, always on the verge of laughter. After dark or in bad weather, Joelle kept close track of Earl and where he might be working.

One afternoon, Earl drove her up on the ridge and parked where they had a view of the entire valley and the mountains beyond. He showed her a parcel of land he was thinking to sell and pointed out the farmsteads where his aunts had lived.

"That's Aunt Lucy's house," he said, pointing at a tiny, gray farmhouse. "She's eighty-nine."

"That's where Aunt Essie lived. Course she's gone now."

"Myrtle lived down by the creek. She went to the home."

He told her these things with a sparkle in his eye, but it wasn't until they were bumping down the ridge road that she guessed. She couldn't quite match up the generations, but the "aunts" must have been his grandfather's wives.

When her husband left, she stayed alone on the ranch. By Christmas, snow had closed the driveway and wind had piled drifts higher than the house. No one came or went, not even Earl, who was busy with his twenty grandchildren.

Each evening, she chopped wood, splitting frozen logs with a maul. People say so often that women have no upper body strength, women themselves come to believe it. But it's a strength that comes of practice. When she'd first come to the ranch, she couldn't *lift* the maul, much less hoist it over her head and bring it down in just the way to split a log with a single cracking blow.

She loaded the wood on a children's plastic sled and

dragged it to the house, carrying enough for a day or two inside, where she stacked it near the stove to dry. In the morning, she pulled on her jacket and knelt before the fire. Her husband had started fires with charcoal lighter, a practice she hated because it made the house smell like a gas station. But the cold had driven out of her all pretense of style. She twisted newspapers, balanced a tent of kindling, and piled on logs. She squirted on charcoal lighter and threw in a match. The fire sometimes went up in a blaze, but most mornings, she had to kneel and feed it kindling, blowing on the coals. Outside, the temperature might be twenty below. Inside, she shivered and stood as close to the fire as she dared, drinking hot coffee.

She managed by herself. Shoveling snow, chopping wood, digging the mailbox out of drifts. It was impossible to walk during the winter. Often, the road sheeted over with blue ice, and the snow drifted so deep she couldn't wade through it. When they still had cattle, she'd once walked out to feed them, balancing on the tops of fence rails.

To get out of the house, she'd learned to ski. Not very well, but well enough to pole out into the pastures where snow covered the fence wire. She liked to follow the tiny herringbone tracks of mice, to see where and how far they might go. Often, they led to lovely, wild wing shapes, each feather perfectly embossed in the snow. The killing marks of an eagle or a hawk.

She was skiing when she saw the moose. She had poled down to the river where willows and stunted trees made a park she could wander in—looking for the larger tracks of foxes and coyotes. The moose stood at some distance, behind a wide golden willow, only its black rump and crooked hind leg visible. "Moose," she thought, "are visually inexplicable."

But moose are dangerous as well. She began to backtrack quietly, to turn and slide one long ski, then the other, over small drifts and around trickling, icy streams. Though she'd arrived in a roundabout way, she wasn't far from the road. She bent her knees and crouched to glide down a steep slope without falling and nearly ran into the moose calf, bedded down under a willow.

"Oh no," she thought. She turned and poled as hard as she could, creating a heartbreakingly short distance between herself and the calf. She heard the mother crashing behind. She tried to make it to the next thick willow stand, but the mother was too close. She turned and tried to kick out of her skis.

The moose stood not ten feet away, its head down, panting in loud snorts, froth dripping from its open mouth. It seemed eight feet tall, and when the animal charged, there was nothing she could do. Not until the moose was right on her did she realize it couldn't see her very well. She side-stepped like a matador, and the moose crashed past. But before she could turn, the moose charged again. Something huge struck her from behind and buckled her knees. She fell into the snow and lay still. But the moose kept charging. The huge, cloven hooves descended again and again, and she could hear her own ribs cracking, the terrible snorting, the frantic woofing sound.

As animals do, the moose suddenly stopped. But it didn't go away. It stood knee-deep in the snow and watched, alert and agitated. She thought, "I'll just lie here for a while." She rested with her head in the snow, glad to be quiet in the still world. She noticed how the snow glistened close to her face. She tried to move just slightly, but pain so severe it twisted her bowels stopped her short. Sweat beaded her forehead, but she wasn't worried. Some sense of a moment's reprieve left her feeling softened and peaceful. The very worst had happened, and she wasn't dead. She waited, wondering how long it would be before the moose attacked again, or the cold seeped all the way into her bones.

Normally, Earl watched her house and telephoned if he saw so much as an out-of-state license plate in her driveway. "See you've got company," he'd say, and wait for her to fill him in. She had avoided telling Earl about the divorce until it was final. Mormons don't believe in it—and she worried. A man his age might think harshly of her. But there was no way he wouldn't notice that only her outfit was parked in the yard. Finally, he caught her at the mailbox, stopped his truck, and climbed out.

"What is it," he inquired, "another woman?"

"Oh Earl," she said, "it's much more serious than that."

"Well, a person has to wonder."

"Earl," she said, "are you going to be this nosy when I'm a single lady?"

"Well, yes," he said, "somebody's got to watch out for you." His *yes* came out in two slow syllables.

. . .

She might have drifted into shock or sleep. When she opened her eyes, the moose and calf were gone. The white world was entirely still. She nearly smiled, hearing Earl's voice and wondering, "Why isn't he looking out for me *now?*" She couldn't tell if she was bleeding. When she made an effort to turn, the pain—like another live animal—attacked her. She spoke to it, as she would to a stubborn horse.

"Quit," she said. "I'm moving now. You cut it out." Slowly, holding on to the pain itself, she turned on her side. Sweat broke out again on her forehead, and nausea turned in her stomach. She rested.

She thought about the way Earl talked to horses, murmuring encouragement and soft corrections, his hands on their hides all the time. When she'd first met him, she was not quite sure he approved of her, or she of him. They had been down at the corrals working heifers, a procedure that required a special language she loved, gentle euphemisms to avoid any mention of sex. To breed a cow was to "freshen" her. A pregnant cow was said to have "settled."

When a cow crashed through the holding pen, one of

Earl's sons drove home and returned with a board and a can of fencing spikes. As he backed up to the rough corral, she heard Earl say, "Honey, you'll have to bear a little to the left." He called his grown sons "honey."

She turned onto her stomach, scolding the pain. "You quit that. Stop right there." "Goddamnit," she said, no longer able to hold back tears. Trying to orient herself, she saw one fiberglass ski splintered into thready pieces. Could she crawl to the road? She wasn't sure how far it was—she had glimpsed it just before she stumbled on the moose calf—but no one would ever see her where she was, her faded jeans and powder-blue down coat would disappear like shadows in the snow.

"Sleepy," she thought. "The sun is making me sleepy." She thought about the many times she'd imagined herself walking out on a fight with her husband. Just wading out into the snow. The easiest of suicides, both guaranteed and painless.

Despite the pain and the fear of causing her body more harm, she crawled. She made some progress where the moose had trampled down the snow. When she rested, she remembered the days and nights she'd spent curled up in her bed after the divorce, crying until she was exhausted. Voices came incessantly, telling her how she had failed. In the darkness, she saw herself as an evil pariah who had always driven everyone away. But those thoughts were not the worst. There came a night when she went down a list of every person she had ever loved, and felt nothing.

For a time, she stopped all thought. It might have been the cold, or shock, but the pain seemed to move off to a safe distance and hover, waiting but not moving in. She all but swam through drifts, thinking she must resemble an enormous turtle inching her way from the sea to lay eggs in the sand.

Deliberately, she began to recall the end of winter, the first days of spring. The times she'd walked down to the river to watch the blue sheets of ice break from the bank and drift down the center of the waterway. There was a sound to it, a slight detonation as each sheet gave way. She remembered the sound of birds calling. The first notes of red-winged blackbirds so sweet after the long winter.

She'd been down at the river one day in early spring help-ing Earl doctor a calf. When they finished, she heard a sound she'd never heard before, a miniature squeak emanating from the river.

"What's that sound?" she asked.

"Birds," he said. "I think it's just birds."

While they waited to see how the calf would respond to the injection, she heard the high peeping again and walked to the bank to look in the water.

"I don't think it's birds," she said. "What is it?"

Earl had lived on this river all his life. Raised his first dairy herd just across the road from where they stood. He would know all the sounds on the river.

Staring into the water, she finally located the source of the sound. Muskrats. The tiny squeaks were coming from muskrats, swirling near the surface—playing and mating. She called Earl over.

He studied the water, blushed, and quickly turned away.

"Well," he said, "in all my years, that's a thing I never saw before."

. . .

It was hours before she reached the edge of the road. Judging from the light, she thought it must be two or three o'clock, close to dark. She crawled out near the bridge where the snowplow hadn't scraped up a mountain of snow to climb over.

Watching for headlights in the distance, she warmed herself again, pretending it was spring, and she noticed how, living alone, she'd come to talk like this to herself, all the time. "Such a busy, private life," she thought.

She remembered standing out at the fence with Earl, watching the spring calves when the grass was tall and green, a luxurious green filled with light. They just stood there visiting, commenting on the weight of one calf, the satisfying block shape of another. One evening, they stood at the gate talking cows and fences for an hour, a soft wind blowing back their jackets and cooling their cheeks. She felt herself expand, as if the wind had lifted and filled her like a sail on a windmill. This is what people mean, she thought, when they tell you, "That day, we were happy." She could not remember ever feeling just that way before.

.   .   .

Earl and his wife came to visit her in the hospital. Her ribs were taped so tightly she could barely speak and couldn't laugh at all. His wife, though plump and in her late sixties, was so beautiful, it was clear she had been quite a catch. They visited, Earl standing a little back, awkward in a sparkling-white shirt and his Sunday hat.

She had vowed, as she crawled out of the snow, that she would tell him how much she loved him. How, though they only saw each other as if by accident, in passing, he had taught her what it was to feel delight. As far as she could recall, Earl was the only older man who had ever liked her.

Instead, they talked about the weather; forty below the night before.

"Good thing you picked a warm day to go skiing," Earl said. "You might have caught your death of cold."

Though laughter brought stinging tears to her eyes, she said: "I should have called you on the phone. 'Earl, there's *a moose* down in the field.'"

"You ask me," Earl said, "had to have been more than one."

NIGHTCRAWLER

Bob and I were waiting at the back of the line in the post office when I heard one of our neighbors, a frail white-haired woman, exclaim in disgust, "They'd catch a rattlesnake and let it go. Those people *won't kill anything*." It took a moment for me to realize "those people" meant us.

The summer before, Bob and I had driven north on a narrow road between dry farms, low swelling hills of ripe grain turning from gold to a roasted brown. We were going fishing. It hadn't rained in more than sixty days, and we had no hay to bale, no grain to cut. We swept to the top of a rise and saw below the entire county laid out, rich furrows of earth where crops had been plowed under. We were waiting to see if the governor would declare a disaster so we could apply for aid, money to buy hay. Nobody held out much hope, and Bob would hardly talk about it.

When we reached the creek, we bumped down a track through the field and parked above the canyon. Bob lifted his fly rod and two rods with rusty reels from the pickup bed, and I carried the cooler down to the water. The creek is wide at that point, sheltered by steep, timbered banks. That day, the water was so clear I could see green, rounded stones, a bed of native jade.

I had talked Bob into fishing with worms. Earlier, a neighbor who stopped by with the drought report told us the fish were biting on Ditch Creek. The water level had been so low all summer, nobody was catching fish, and I think by that time, even Bob thought he was losing his touch.

Bob fishes with flies and barbless hooks and never brings home a fish, but I had told him I didn't want to go fishing, I wanted to eat a fish. A trout right from the water. "Heming-way," I said, "fished with worms." When he finally gave in, I packed a crusted black iron skillet and plates. He dug his tackle box and fishing rods out of the shed while I packed the truck with a cooler of Coke and beer and managed to find a can of mosquito repellent—the only thing we really couldn't leave without. I found an empty coffee can and a trowel and walked out to the part of the garden I'd been able to water that morning.

Bob followed me and hovered in the background, suddenly quiet. Something about his posture told me I had to stop and pry the problem out of him. I stood and walked to where he leaned on a fence post, his hands in his pockets. The sun was on the west side of the sky, and we didn't have much time if we were going to get to the creek by evening.

"What's the matter?" I asked him. "Changed your mind?"

"No."

"Well, we need to go then."

"I know," he said, but he didn't move. It took some time, but finally I dragged it out of him. Bob didn't want to kill the worms. Apparently, it was okay to buy worms, but not to sacrifice your own. I shook my head and went along with Bob, but I was annoyed. What was he thinking, farm-raised worms were something like ranch-raised mink? He acted like he knew the worms personally.

On the drive north, I teased him. "Couldn't we just call ours free-range worms?" Bob managed a grin. "Milk-fed worms?" got a laugh. I watched the side of the road for a hand-painted sign for nightcrawlers. All gardeners like worms, but more so where six feet of snow compacts the ground all winter; they loosen the soil and mean the earth is rich and healthy. When I turned the garden in the spring and fall, I was careful not to harm the worms. But I thought Bob was going too far. I thought, "What kind of hypocrite would raise beef cows and not kill worms?" Finally, we stopped at a house with a hand-painted sign and bought a pint container from a tow-headed boy with a raw, pink, sunburned nose.

I agreed to fish downstream from Bob, and when he was out of sight behind the willows at a bend in the stream, I selected a worm and realized I was going to have to pinch it into smaller pieces. Instead, I managed to wrap the enormous worm around my hook, struggling and thinking, "Double half hitch." The line seemed almost too heavy to cast but I managed to swing it like a pendulum across the creek and into the shadow of a willow. When I reeled the line in, the worm was gone.

I'd thought fishing with bait would be a snap. I'd catch a fish on every cast. But the fish just weren't biting. They weren't even rising. The sun struck the surface of the water in sheets of molten gold so bright they hurt my eyes. When I looked away, shadows darkened the bank, and I could hardly see my tackle bag.

I gave up and began to walk upstream, negotiating the slippery creek bed in my sneakers and watching the water flow over stones. Some were the color of turquoise and others a deep vegetable green. From time to time, I bent down and collected one or two.

Nearly hypnotized by the sun and the moving water, I remembered an event I hadn't thought about in years, probably not since it happened. When I was a teenager, I had an enormous white tomcat. You could see him slinking down the driveway, his ears flat and only his feet moving, like a centipede. Both ears were battle scarred when we got him, and my mother called him Poor White Trash. My little sister named him Snow.

Whenever my grandmother came by, the first thing she saw was Snow, lounging on the dining-room table. My mother never heard the end of this unsanitary situation, but it didn't bother us. We all loved that cat.

I must have been in high school, because I was driving. When I got home from school, my mother was already there, early for some reason. She cornered me in the dining room and told me the cat had been in another fight, his ear was split, and he needed stitches, but she wasn't going to pay for another trip to the vet. She made me take the cat to the vet and have him put to sleep.

Standing in the creek with water flowing past my ankles, I thought, "I was shy then and awkward, but still, how can anybody make you do a thing like that? Why didn't I protest?" I don't think I even told my brother and sister. I don't think I told anybody.

I remembered exactly how I felt when I drove to the animal hospital with tears just under the surface, in a state of sadness so familiar, I thought it was my personality.

But until that moment walking in the water, I'd never thought what my mother did was cruel. I'd never seen myself as a child, or thought of my mother as a parent whose job was to protect her children from that kind of harm.

Because my brother and sister stayed for sports, I was always the first one home from school, and I'd be the one to discover that we had no lights because my mother hadn't paid the bill. I was twelve when I started answering the phone in the hall and had to listen to the bill collectors yell at me, threatening to send my mother to jail. When I was older, I made the calls myself as soon as I got home, trying to persuade the strangers on the line to turn the water or the heat back on.

When the sun left the canyon and the river in shadow, I hiked back up to the truck and waited for Bob. On the drive home I helped Bob drink the beer. He hadn't caught a fish, and an old anger rose in me. It was so much easier, I wanted to tell him, to be sad for animals than to be sad for people. Bob cared about every animal he came across, but it never made him think ahead. His big heart never got the hay baled or the mortgage paid.

We pulled into the driveway after dark, and the night was suddenly freezing. I shivered and ran for the house. Bob brought in the cooler and fishing gear before he walked into the front room and sank onto the couch. When he turned on the TV, I could hear the news. The governor had declared a drought emergency. "You hear that?" he hollered, and went for the phone.

I opened the cooler, retrieved the pint container of worms and let myself out the back door. Though the air was icy, I walked to the end of the garden where the soil might still be damp and pried off the lid. Kneeling, I poured the worms out onto the ground and watched them scramble to uncurl.

"Run," I said. "The governor just called."

OPOSSUM

The Florida summer was so thick with humid heat and singing mosquitos, the women reclined on the screened porch tipping vodka into glasses of iced tea. They worried about late alimony checks and complained of the boredom of staying home with kids. The older of the two, her yellow capris cupping a small potbelly, used one finger to slide butterfly eyeglasses up on a pinched, ski-jump nose. The younger woman, her thick, auburn hair swept up from her neck in a knotted bandana, wiped perspiration from her brow and wished for air-conditioning.

"Where are the kids?" the older woman asked.

"Outside. Playing." The woman was vague.

"In this heat?"

"Where's Alicia?"

"When I left, she pretended she was sleeping. Fourteen is a tedious age."

The younger woman lifted the skirt of her housedress to fan her face, revealing long, slender legs. "If we had any money, we could be in Cuba now, lying on the beach. . . . God, even the kids are bored. They wander around the house all summer, asking, 'What is there to do?'" She laughed. "I'd like to ship them all off to a nice air-conditioned orphanage."

The children had set out at dawn when a mist cooled their bare feet and shrouded ancient oaks that dripped with Spanish moss and floating vines. They made their way, two girls and a boy, across one vacant lot, then another, angling toward the bay. Each one wore a pair of faded shorts and a striped T-shirt.

They detoured around the oak-shaded country club, the stables and white, slatted fences where rich girls posted by on glistening, high-stepping horses, and entered the jungle of trees and palmettos again. The path wandered, and along the way they passed places where the hanging vines made perfect tents, tepees they had explored in the past. They skirted Indian burial mounds, where the sandy earth, the color of sweet potatoes, had been excavated into pits by treasure hunters and came to a halt to watch a blacksnake, four feet long, slither away from their feet.

Lucy, who was ten, the older of the two girls, leapt and made a snatch for the neck of the snake, but caught it too far back, where the snake, though harmless, could turn and bite her. She tossed it gently, a long black whip looping into the brush.

At the bay, the parking lot had filled with cars, and men with fishing hats and tackle boxes ambled toward the pier. The children walked in single file onto the splintered planks, silver fish scales sticking to the bottoms of their feet, alert for rusty hooks and shards of glass.

At the end of the pier, a small crowd had gathered around a man holding something alive. They crept close and saw that he held an opossum by the tail. Even dangling over the pier, the opossum pretended she was sleeping, curled up on herself.

Lucy watched in fascination. The opossum, pale gray, its belly almost white with pink skin underneath, was the softest, sweetest thing she'd ever seen. She wanted to reach out and stroke it. The man in dirty khaki pants and shirt, his hands almost black with grime, reached into the opossum's pouch and pinched out a tiny baby. All the children stepped back. The man cupped the little comma of a baby in his huge, black hand. It looked unnatural, prehistoric or unborn.

"Look," the man said. "It's alive. It lives in there."

Holding the one baby back in his palm, he reached into the pouch and showed them another.

Lucy felt a terrible alarm, a fear that something very dark was happening. She stepped forward and held out both small palms. The man looked at her and at her open hands. He didn't know what to do. They all waited while he held the opossum's rat tail in one fist, the tiny babies in the other. Finally he placed each baby in her hands, as if he were a miser making change with precious coins.

The opossum's long snout filled with pink gums and sharp, razor teeth. She curled up on herself, hissing, and struck the hand that held her. Blood swelled from the man's hand, and wet streams of red poured down his fingers and splashed on his boots. He swung and threw the opossum into the bay.

Lucy ran, the tiny babies cupped against her chest, against her sweaty shirt. She ran until a stitch pierced her side. She ducked into a tent inside the vines and sank into a crouch. Her brother and sister caught up to her. Her sister, only four, held out her hands.

"Let *me* see . . . I want to see, too."

Lucy cautiously uncurled her palm, just enough for all of them to see. "They can't live without their mom," she said.

"The mom swam," her brother said. "I saw her swim."

They huddled close together, making plans: "We'll get a cage. A good stick. We'll find the mom. She won't bite us. We can raise the babies by ourselves. We'll make a box."

A slight breeze lifted as the sun went down behind the oaks. The women felt reprieved. With the air came the tingle of an old excitement, of bare shoulders and summer evenings on the arms of men in uniform. When they heard the screen door slam, they both stopped speaking in mid-word.

"Little pitchers have big ears," the younger said.

The three children wandered into the room, their eyes averted and their arms hanging useless at their sides. Their feet were nicked and muddy, and their clothes and hair were damp. Sweat beads encircled the folds of their necks. "When's supper?" they wanted to know.

Their mother sipped from her glass of tea. "Go back out and play," she said. "The adults are talking."

The children sprang for the door, as if released from a spell.

Their mother gazed into the cooling dusk, her face softened to a wistful beauty by drink and recollection. "During the war," she said, "I had an off-the-shoulder gown, yards and yards of taffeta with pink lining. Japanese silk lining, the color of rosebuds."

PORCUPINE

Who can say why I slept with the cowboy—a married
man with children. I knew he was married. I had met
his wife and kids. He knew, better than I did, that my
old boyfriend loved me, that he would be harmed. I
could say we had too much to drink, or that the end of
summer felt like the end of my childhood.

Maybe it was because I loved everything about the
west: icy mornings under huge, blue skies, the smell of
cut alfalfa, the way plump heifers look, their ankles

white and thick, like teenagers' in bobby socks. Wyoming drew me . . . in the way young boys awaken to the tingling of the body, or young women lie in bed and dream of dancing in the dark.

After college, I followed an old boyfriend, Ray, to Wyoming and worked as a cook at a guest ranch. He worked on a cattle ranch owned by the same family, flood-irrigating fields of old alfalfa, swathing hay, fixing fence, and moving cattle. One evening in August, as the ranch wife drove me back from town, the van filled with groceries, we saw a straggling band of elk cross the road and disappear into a grove of aspen trees. My boss stopped the van and climbed out. She gave a horn-like call that whistled the elk right out of the trees. Until that moment, I hadn't understood how wild animals wandered around in the mountains on their own. I don't know what I thought before. They lived in Africa, or zoos?

I cooked three meals a day, six days a week, for forty guests, and though I came to hate the dark log buildings, the press of people and the lack of privacy, there was time after dinner to ride bareback up into the hills. There was time to drive the forty miles to town and dance in every bar. On Friday nights, the hay crew at the cattle ranch unpacked clean shirts, showered in the corner of the tractor shed, and pulled on new boots.

Ray and I were children of the sixties, and though we never spent the night together, everybody thought we did. We drove the back roads into town, and I danced while he drank beer in one bar after another.

When it came time to brand the breeding herd, the pure-bred cows that weren't up on the range, help came from Utah, a man and his wife and their three small boys. When the wife tried to help in the pens, the women at the ranch house vilified her, "What's she think she's doing, out there in a miniskirt?" The air in the old, tar-shingled house was always warm and close with the sweet-sour smells of damp oilcloth and thick cream from the dairy cow.

The wife and children went home to their own small ranch, but the husband, a wiry, dark-haired man in his early thirties, stayed on to help with the last cut of hay. Ray had been the head of the hay crew until then, but as if by silent agreement, the older man took over. His name was Bill Williams, and behind his back, the crew good-naturedly called him the double Bill. The summer was ending. Already, the days were growing shorter.

Ray and I saddled horses under a gray sky and rode to the Snake River to look for moose and eagles—with ice and snow pitting our hands and cheeks. The land flowed in glaciated plains, high benches spotted with sagebrush, and the mountains rose straight up from the valley floor. Wandering near the river, I found a round, dark-stained rock, a piece of petrified palm. Afterward, I couldn't think of this place without knowing swamps had been there and wondering how it looked to early trappers. Someone had to be the first to wander into Yellowstone. What would they have told back home about mineral pools the color of morning glories and boiling water shooting up out of the ground?

After the guests had gone for the year, I couldn't bring myself to leave. I borrowed a tent and pitched it up a canyon beside a narrow creek that, in those days, ran so clear I could drink from it. One of the cowboys had seen a black bear not far from my camp, and at night I lay awake, afraid to fall asleep. I would never have told anyone I was terrified. The mountains were alive with breaking twigs, small feet, water rushing over deadfall. When I finally closed my eyes, I slept on into the peaceful, sun-filled mornings—the daylight bringing a false sense of safety. I awoke knowing I had dreamed about Bill Williams. What is it that draws us to certain men and not others? Bill chewed tobacco, but he had an angle to his mouth, a way of speaking in a dry, western accent with the consonants worn down.

On the last Friday night, when nearly all the hay was baled and stacked, I showered in the tractor shed before the hay crew quit work for the day. I'd brought with me a sheer, white cowboy shirt and my last pair of washed and folded jeans. I waited while Ray cleaned up, and we drove his pickup the long way into town. We were driving slowly along the base of the mountains, on a twisting, narrow dirt road hoping to see moose or deer, when we heard a peeping squeak, a frantic noise of something hurt or injured coming from the ditch. We stopped the truck in the still evening air and listened. The sound became more urgent, and we climbed out, searching the downed timber beside the road. A porcupine waddled out of the ditch, its barbed tail raised and its spines fanned up so high it looked enormous, the size of a large, bundled coat.

"It's been hit by a car," Ray said.

"Can we do anything?" I stepped cautiously closer.

"Look," Ray said.

I turned back to the ditch and saw the peaked nose of a second porcupine as it swayed onto the road. In its tipping walk, it pursued the first one, and the two began to mate. The female cried again.

Ray backed up toward the truck.

"They're fine," he said. "Let's just give 'em room."

Despite all the jokes about how porcupines make love, as we drove into town, I thought about that sound, the female crying out in pain. At the same time, I felt privileged to have seen such a thing. "It couldn't be that bad," I thought. After all, we see *a lot* of porcupines.

We parked the truck on the town square and walked to the bar where we'd agreed to meet the hay crew. We worked our way through the crowd to an empty table in the back. Ray went for beers.

If I had to tell myself the truth, a thing one never does in courtship, I would have admitted I was waiting for Bill. I was with Ray, but I had dressed and washed my hair for Bill.

.

When Bill arrived, he danced with all the silly maids and cabin girls who were ending the season as I was. Ray slumped in his chair, his mood turning dark with too much beer.

By the time Bill sat down next to me, I'd had too many myself.

"Robbing the cradle?" I said.

"Just trying to," Bill laughed.

The warmth of the beer made me sit too close. I couldn't remember when I'd been that close to a man wearing after-shave. I watched his mouth as he spoke to me.

"We're just going down to the Rancher," we told Ray, "see what the band's like." Ray nodded, leaning back against the wall.

But we didn't go to the Rancher. We crossed the street to the Cowboy Bar, and in the back, past the bar, past the pool tables and the stuffed wolf and the diorama lights, we danced on the small wooden floor. Bill placed his hand on my back and whispered in my ear, surprised, "You're not wearing a bra. . . ." I held his shaved cheek in my hand.

We never even looked for Ray. Drunk, we drove Bill's

truck out of town, out past the ranch, hardly able to stop touching each other. To this day, truck seats that smell of harness and dust and hay chaff make me wish for that night back. He couldn't believe I would go to bed with him—that I had a tent or thought he was handsome. He confided that he thought maybe one of the girls would go for him—but not me. I was better than he was—too educated, too refined.

The tent was freezing. We stripped out of our clothes and snaked into my sleeping bag. I wanted simply to mold my body into his and kiss his crooked mouth. His body was like no other I had ever felt. Bucking hay had turned his muscles so hard, they had no give. His shoulders and arms seemed made of wood.

Bill fell asleep with his heavy arm across my chest, and I lay awake for a long time, marveling at the weight of it, the density of muscle. The gesture of holding me seemed so intimate, so tender. For the first time in weeks, I fell asleep in safety, unafraid.

Bill awoke very early and drove me down to the ranch. We hardly spoke. He went to work, the last day of stacking hay, and loaded his truck to drive home. In the late afternoon, I met him briefly in Ray's room at the bunkhouse.

He stood there in a white T-shirt, his face and arms dark with sweat and hay dust. He seemed like a boy with narrow hips and rounded arms and shoulders.

In an almost courtly way, he said to me, "I came in earlier and told Ray I was sorry."

I kissed him on the cheek and stepped away, as if we were only kind travelers, each on our way. But I wondered, "Why had he apologized to Ray, and not to me?" There were rules in operation here, but I didn't know just what they were, what kind of honor was at stake.

I couldn't stay in the west. There was no place for me. I couldn't stand the way women were treated—how all the wives stayed in the kitchen and told great, funny stories about the men, who had wider lives. Ray never spoke to me again. He took another job in Wyoming, and I can't remember what it was about the west, about hard, dirty work, that seemed so glamorous to me. When I packed my car to leave, I was surprised at how little there was to take with me.

But if I tell the truth, I know why I slept with Bill. As I drove the winding road above the steep gorge of the river, I thought, "There is no adventure like the first touch of a man, the skin on skin, the nakedness of strangers."

QUAIL

Pequod, aged as she was, hunched for hours in front of the plate-glass window, watching for rabbits and doves. At fourteen, she resembled a moth-eaten fur piece tossed in a heap. Only when she moved did the bone shape of a cat emerge.

My husband had just been given tenure, and we'd bought a small house on the mesa, in the Chihuahuan Desert of New Mexico, just north of the Mexican border. Tiny rabbits flounced through the yard unimpeded by the cyclone fence that circled the property, and doves murmured in the elderberry trees. The view across the green Rio Grande Valley to the mountains drew us the way the doves drew Pequod to the windows. We had our own oasis.

I didn't like to admit I was afraid at night when my husband was teaching late or away at a conference. We would have looked for a dog, but my husband had promised Pequod no dogs or other pets until she died, and I had agreed. Despite her arthritic state, she could still manage to leap onto the couch and stretch out on a heated pad. I bought her a magnet bed—and drove her into town for acupuncture treatments.

As ridiculous as it seemed to me to take a cat for acupuncture, the treatments helped. I kept taking her even after the vet, a neighbor on the mesa, looked up from his needles and demanded to know, "Is your house defensible?"

Stumped, I waited to find out what on earth he meant.

"You know, can you defend it from attack?"

"Attack from *whom*?"

"The millennium is coming," he said. It turned out he was hoarding guns and food, not half a mile from us. He believed that, as the century turned, all 1.2 million Mexicans in Juárez would go berserk and swarm across the border. I hardly let my husband in the house that night before I told him the whole story.

"Is our house *defensible?*" I laughed. "The whole house is made of glass."

"Didn't I tell you?" he said. "I *ordered* the howitzer. We'll mount it on the roof."

"What do you think the vet thinks the hordes are going to *do?*"

"Our whole way of life will be destroyed," he said. "They'll force us to *eat better*. We'll have to be nicer to our children."

"No more heart attacks," I said.

Two weeks later, we came home from dinner with friends to find we had been robbed. We hadn't been gone long, and at first we couldn't figure out quite what was wrong. We saw the computer, dropped just inside the door, and still we weren't sure what had happened, why things seemed so odd.

When we finally took it in, we made a frantic search for Pequod, terrified she might be dead or gone, lost out in the desert. We found her backed into the bottom of a closet, hissing like a young, healthy cat. It took my husband hours, holding her on his lap, to calm her.

I started the sad inventory. Everything that could be carried and sold was gone. It could not have happened at a worse time. My mother had died the year before, and I had just that week taken her things out of storage. The silver was gone. Jewelry she'd promised to me since I was a girl. Photographs in silver frames. The stereo and television. Even the telephone was gone. Later, my husband had to hike next door to call the sheriff.

We hired workmen to fix the smashed back window. In the following days, friends from the university brought us a telephone and a television set. Everybody made suggestions: We were offered the loan of everything from pit bulls to attack geese.

Eventually, we were forced to lock our gates and install iron grids on all the windows, and Pequod stayed well away. If we went out, we returned to find her hiding again in the closet. Though the winter was not severe, we suffered the short days and early darkness. We talked about moving into

town. We lit fires in the stove and huddled at night, holding
Pequod, feeling like prisoners in our own house.

I still thought the vet was nuts—although, the day of the
robbery, a strange truck had been seen in our neighborhood,
driven by dark-skinned boys. I continued to transport Pequod
to her treatments, but the cat did not respond. At home, we
had to lift her, nearly weightless, onto the couch and, watching her try to walk, I felt as if I could see her dry bones, the
frail skeleton that didn't fit together anymore.

The sheriff had told me to look in antique stores and
pawnshops for my jewelry, for my mother's silver. I forced
myself to go one day, and in a narrow shop crowded with
glass cases of shimmering teapots and engraved trays, I discovered four spoons that had been ours. When the police met
me there, the proprietor, a cigarette stub hanging from his
dry lip, gave up the spoons—but not the names of who had
sold them. I knew he must have bought more . . . but he
refused to look. He showed us dusty boxes jumbled full of
tangled bracelets and rings and pins. "Look all you want," he
said to me. Two patrolmen stood there while we went
through this charade.

I was so filled with fury, I thought I shouldn't even drive the car, but I made it home. At the house, my key stuck in the wrought-iron door we'd had installed over the glass one. I thought, "I'm going to kick it in. I'm going to have to break into my own damn house."

When I finally won my battle with the lock, I called my husband at his office and railed at him, at the sly proprietor, at the police, at the world at large. In his good way, he listened to me yell, not saying, "What did you expect?" Not saying, "There, there, it's all right." Nothing was right, and he knew it, too.

Exhausted, I didn't think to look for Pequod. I lay down on the couch, my feet on her heating pad, and cried. I cried until the bones in my face hurt, and then, deliberately, I fell into the refuge of sleep.

When I awoke, afternoon light poured through the windows. I made myself a cup of tea and went to look for Pequod. She wasn't in the closet. I searched under the beds and in the other closets, growing more and more alarmed. "If we lose her because of the burglars," I thought, "I'll track them down and shoot them all myself."

I only chanced to look out the glass door. The iron grid stood open, and my husband was sitting on the patio, gazing over the adobe wall at the mountains. He looked so young to me, sitting there. He seemed to be smiling.

As I approached the door, he sensed me there and held a finger to his lips. I slid the door open slowly and stepped out. The air was unseasonably warm. He had Pequod on his lap, and both of them were staring, riveted, it seemed to me, by nothing. As I watched, a quail hurried along the top of the wall. He was so close, we could see his headdress—like a silly hat a woman in the forties might have worn. The stem curled from his forehead and on the end, a black, velvet teardrop bobbed ahead.

I had never seen a quail so close before. We all watched him flush from the wall and disappear on the other side. I started to speak, and my husband held up his hand. I watched Pequod. Her mouth chattered with an old instinct, her gray whiskers shivering. We watched as another quail, and another, followed the first along the wall and off into the desert. An entire family of quail bobbled past, making clicking sounds back and forth as if intent on private business.

My husband rose and, ferrying Pequod ahead of him in both palms, returned her to the heating pad. One knobby limb at a time, she stretched out, still a moth-eaten fur piece forgotten on the couch, and we could hear her purr, a tiny, rusted engine. We opened all the grates and bars on all the windows and sat until the sun cast shadows on the mountains and went down. We sat beside the sleeping cat—the great hunter—all evening, talking quietly amongst ourselves.

RED PONY

A wind had come up and the weather turned cold, and while two men loaded her station wagon with dog food and burlap bags of wild-bird seed, Helena read the cards and notices overlapped on the bulletin board, intrigued by offers of free goats, horseshoeing, earth-moving. She waited in the warm, dusty office, examining glossy color photographs of stallions standing at stud and desperate messages scrawled on the backs of receipts: "Green broke colt must go." Each time she'd waited in the office, she'd seen a business card for Don

Juan Ranch, Tennessee Walking Horses, with an address not far from her own. She glanced around quickly, pried off the card, and slipped it into her coat pocket, feeling like a shoplifter.

As she turned out of the lot and onto the main road, the rounded tops of white clouds appeared behind the desert peaks of the Franklin Mountains, and despite the probability of rain, she took the long way home along the Rio Grande, passing through one early Spanish town after another— clusters of angular adobe buildings, their thick walls rounded and crumbling with age, every deep, square window glowing with pale Christmas lights. She left the county road, negotiated a series of doglegs back through fallow cotton fields and acres of alfalfa, and turned in to her own driveway. At the front door she braked and gave the horn a tap, alerting Stan to come unload the heavy bags so she could put the car away. She waited in the cold for what seemed plenty of time before she climbed out, extracting an aluminum cane, a new concession to her arthritis.

In the dark house, she found Stan at his computer, his father's bird dog curled at his feet. Tax forms had slid from

his desk to the floor. When she spoke his name, he looked up
and blinked as if, for a moment, he couldn't place her.

"Dog food," she said.

"In a minute." He turned back to the charts and tables on
his monitor.

Helena left the wagon where it was and walked along the
hall, turning on lights as she went, to the living room. The
week before, she'd unpacked a lifetime of collected ornaments, hung them on a fresh piñon pine, and arranged
beneath it packages wrapped in shining paper. Every year,
she looked forward to the pleasure of sitting on the couch as
she had as a girl, taking in the clean, new smell of the ever-
green tree and watching the lights gleam in softened shades
of red and green and gold. Though the packages under the
tree were not for her, their abundance reminded her of the
wise men bearing gifts, of the practice of bestowing gifts on
strangers, ambassadors or heads of state.

She was ashamed that she still wanted gifts for herself.
Like a child, she waited in anticipation, watching as parcels
arrived in the mail from her family, and gazing at them
under the tree, wondering what they might contain. Though

he did it at the last minute, somehow Stan always managed to see that she had an abundance of presents to open on Christmas morning.

As she sat in the living room waiting for Stan to unload the car, she carried her thoughts forward to the disappointment, the sudden emptiness that invaded her after the packages were opened and the papers and ribbons scattered on the floor. It wasn't only that the anticipation, the decorating and Christmas cooking were over, it was a sudden blow that always felled her. After so many years, she still couldn't understand why Stan and her family gave her gifts she would never use, perfumes she would never wear, books she wouldn't read, heavy ornaments for someone else's house. Sometimes she and Stan did laugh. How many trivets could a person use in one lifetime?

She traced this feeling, this emptiness, to a day just before her fifth birthday. Her father had taken her along on a sales trip to Biloxi, Mississippi, and driven her into the country to visit an old friend. On the way, he taught her "Goodnight Irene," because the friend was named Irene. While her dark-haired, handsome father remained in the house, she wandered outside, examining with fascination the stone well, the first she'd ever seen, and watching as one by one a small herd of shaggy ponies with heavy manes and soft, dished-in faces drifted to the fence across the road to look at her. Later, as they were all saying goodbye, she pointed out the horses to her father and asked him if she could have a horse like that.

"Sure you can," her father said.

Helena had believed him so unquestioningly that she waited through every birthday and every Christmas for the horse to appear. Though she seldom saw her father—once when she was twelve, and not again until her twenties—she expected the horse to appear.

In her teens, she managed to join a riding club and take lessons, meanwhile carting home every book in the library that might have to do with horses, until she brought home a book called *The Red Pony*. She was drawn deeply into this story of a boy who is surprised by the gift of a red pony. She studied all the details of how the boy learned to feed and brush the pony, how he was given a precious red saddle, how his life was transformed. When the pony, left out in the rain by accident, fell sick, she suffered through all the details of how the boy rubbed his hide with burlap sacks, fed him hot mash, and finally had to let the hired man take a sharp knife and cut a hole in the pony's windpipe.

She was so sure these measures would save the pony, it came as a slap to her, a harsh surprise when—less than halfway through the book—the pony died. She felt angry and betrayed. How could they call a book *The Red Pony* and let the pony die? She returned the book unfinished to the library and never checked out another book on horses.

The spring before, Stan's father had died, leaving him to manage his mother's affairs. Always a private man, he'd withdrawn more deeply into himself. After the summer passed and the days began to grow shorter, she started to dream again, as she had as a girl, of horses. In the dreams, she rode the ranch in Wyoming with Stan's father, who was always showing her places, warm springs and buffalo wallows that she'd never known were there. But the dreams that woke her were dreams of black horses.

In the dreams, she was astride a galloping black stallion, terrified the horse would step in a burrow, a badger hole, and throw her. She would fall, and the horse would fall on top of her, breaking her bones. She tried to slow the horse, but he ran harder, flattening to the ground, and it occurred to her to lay herself down on his neck, to cling like a jockey until she felt they were one creature. They were safe then because if they fell, they would fall together, and neither would be hurt.

Helena shifted on the couch, stiff from sitting too long in front of the tree. Holding her back, she lifted herself from the couch like a pregnant woman, and decided to risk entering Stan's sanctum again to remind him of the feed sacks.

Stan said, "I'll get to it."

Helena retreated. Stan was assembling tax receipts, theirs as well as his mother's, not a job she would welcome herself. In the past, she would have unloaded the wagon without him, but now it was all she could manage to retrieve the groceries and start to put together dinner. Outside, the wind began to rise, and suddenly drops of rain pelted the skylights above her head.

Rain, she thought. It hadn't rained in months. She opened the wide doors off the foyer and stood in the cooling air. Exhilarated, she moved to the edge of the porch. Limbs in the willows thrashed in the wind, and a branch tore away and landed with a slap of wet leaves at her feet.

Helena went for her raincoat and purse, made her way to the car, and drove out the gate. When the tires slipped and the wagon slithered on the slick mud, she gave it more gas. She climbed up along the base of the mesa and turned at an enormous white sign for Don Juan Ranch. With the feed bags for ballast, she pushed the car to the top and parked in front of a grand, white adobe house. Covering her head with her purse, she ran to the porch.

A trim, blond woman, dressed in teal-colored silk and matching cowboy boots, pink lipstick clinging to her teeth, came to the door.

"Well," she said. "All right." A tiny poodle skittered around her feet. "Go lie down, Flower," she said, her accent sweet and Texan.

The rain had abated somewhat, but darkness was closing. The younger woman handed Helena a hooded slicker, but then she hesitated at the door.

"You're sure you don't want to come back another time?"

"No," Helena assured her. "I'm just fine."

The two women walked from pen to pen, looking at wet, despondent horses, their rumps turned toward the rain. The breeder read prices and bloodlines from a sheet of damp paper.

Helena slowed with the weight of disappointment. These horses were inelegant, with large, ugly heads and square bodies. As the two of them walked, Helena had no trouble saying, no, not that one, no. The breeder asked her if she was sure she didn't want to come back in the morning, see the horses when it wasn't raining. Helena shook her head, and the two women ducked into a cavernous metal barn. In the first box stall, Helena saw a horse she liked, a glistening red stallion, his muscles carved and rippling on his neck.

She had explained to the woman about her arthritis and how she wasn't sure she could ride anymore, but if she could, she thought a Tennessee Walker, a gaited horse with no trot, might help. The breeder nodded and told her about a retired saddle maker who sold his mare, only to find that it hurt just as much to sit in a chair as to sit on a horse.

"Well," the woman said, looking from the stallion to Helena, "every horse on the place is for sale, at a price. Let's look at a few more."

The breeder led her back outside to a pen that stretched out into the sandy desert. She unlatched the gate and waited while Helena followed her in. When she whistled, a smaller black horse appeared, and Helena knew. She knew right then, this would be her horse. The younger woman grasped his halter and rubbed his face with the side of her glove before she stepped around and slapped him on the flank. Though darkness had come, outdoor lights reflected from his shining, arched neck, and as he ran the circuit of his pen, his tail lifted up and swept behind him like a flag.

"He's a lot of horse. They left him a stud until he was ten, and he's only twelve now," the breeder said. "But I've ridden this guy. This horse would never hurt you."

Helena approached the horse and held out her palm. He grazed it with the whiskers on his chin, then nibbled at her coat sleeve. Almost any other horse would have bitten her, but the black gelding lipped his way up her arm and exhaled a warm, sudden breath on her neck.

She didn't even bargain for the horse, as she knew she should. She sat in the office out of the rain and wrote out a check for three thousand dollars. It was her own money, rents from a small acreage she'd kept. They agreed to leave the

horse where he was for the time being. Helena could practice there.

Not until she was driving home on the slick roads in the
dark, slowing to five miles an hour, did she understand this
was not an impulse buy; she'd been planning it, keeping the
plan a secret, even from herself.

In the warm house, Stan sat on the edge of the hearth, a
dark Scotch in his hand, while she sat near the twinkling tree
and told him what she'd done.

Stan's face turned red and seemed to swell.

"What kind of person would do that?" he demanded. She
had never seen him so mad.

"You want a horse?" he nearly shouted, "I'll get you a
horse from the cutters. You don't need any three-thousand-
dollar horse."

He stood up and walked into the kitchen, still raising his
voice. "A good horse shouldn't cost anywhere near like that."

While his back was turned, Helena stood and left the
room. She pulled on old boots and her raincoat and made her
way in the dark to the car. Slowly, she hauled the bags of feed
from the tailgate and levered them into the wheelbarrow.
When she grasped the handles and pushed the front wheel

through the mud, needles of pain shot through her hips, but she ignored them. She pushed the barrow into the shed, all the time thinking, "He's right. I won't ever be able to ride that horse. Stan is right."

But walking back to the house, with the wind tossing the leaves high in the trees, some ancient weight seemed to lift from her shoulders. "I'm fifty-nine years old," she thought. "And I just bought myself a horse." She remembered the feel of warm breath on her neck.

She stopped when she saw the sky had cleared and watched the moon edge over the Franklins, just where they tapered like the tail of an ancient lizard and ended near El Paso, *el paseo del norte*. Stan was always telling people how they'd only moved from the middle of the Rocky Mountains to the end. "Why," she wondered, "do we think the Rockies end here?" She smiled and pictured Spanish soldiers plunging the first western horses into the river. They would not have risked their lives to see the end. These barren rocks were only the beginning.

SIREN

When she heard the sirens on the channel, she stepped cautiously outside in time to see the red and white life-guard boat, radar and blue lights revolving, speeding toward the ocean. Behind it, the sheriff's boat plowed a churning wake, its prow lifted out of the water. After they vanished around the curve of the jetty, she retreated back into her apartment until she heard the heavy, deafening engine of a helicopter thundering off the water, so loud it seemed as if the sound might knock the building down. She stood it as long as she could before she ventured back out on her patio. Above the center of the channel, a green combat helicopter hovered, huge and menacing, like the thorax of a locust.

Her neighbors appeared outside their apartments to stare. When she'd moved in, the wife of the man upstairs had leaned over her balcony to tell her in a tumbling rush of British accent, "Oh, I could never live below. I hate the creepy crawlies. I just couldn't stand the bugs, you know?" Her neighbor to the east, a lovely young lawyer with skin the color of light coffee, had caught her outside and edged over to warn, "Watch out for the rats." She claimed a wharf rat the size of a small dog had chewed through her screen door.

As they all stood on the asphalt path between their apartments and the channel, she heard the neighbor to the west yell into his telephone, demanding that the noise be stopped, the helicopter withdrawn. Though he was a young man, his nose and shoulders and belly had a melted look, as if bitterness had conspired with gravity to shape him like a fig. He had confided to her that he had padded his walk-in closet with moving-van quilts to practice primal screaming.

The couple upstairs leaned over their balcony and called down, "It's on the television." As she strained to hear them, the vessel-assist boat went by, and she saw in tow behind it the canopy of a cabin cruiser, its hull just visible beneath the water.

On her own television, she watched an anchorman interview two men wrapped in blankets, shivering on a dock.

"We were right there," one said, his voice flat with disgust. "We told them to jump." He shook his head in disbelief. "We were close enough to get 'em."

The second man wept. "Most of them jumped, but the last two froze. They wouldn't go. I don't know why."

The first man shook his head. "They waited until it was too late," he said. "The cruiser was going down. I could have fished them from the water."

Both men had jumped into the ocean themselves, the first man diving for the sinking boat. "It went too quick," he said.

According to the anchorman, the lifeguard vessel had arrived in that instant and rescued all the boaters in the water. Divers with air tanks brought up two unconscious people, a woman and a child, and started life support.

. . .

In the morning, her upstairs neighbor was quick to tell her the two people had not survived. The woman and the child had drowned. At the last minute, they had rushed back to cower in the cabin. For days afterward, she overheard her neighbors speculating. "Where were the life jackets?" "Didn't they know how to swim?"

During the night, she had thought about the strangers, the woman and child, hoping they would live. The incident had shaken her and brought her far too close to tears. She had come to the city for therapy herself, for sessions where she tried to explain to different doctors how it had happened. How, alone on the ranch, winter had invaded with darkness. Though she knew better than to lose contact with her friends and neighbors, she had drifted slowly into solitude, her days a stark routine of chopping wood, feeding horses, shoveling snow, thawing pipes.

When she called her father from the hospital, she could tell his mind was blank, he had no idea what to say. After a long silence, he raised his voice, almost shouting, "Well, just get out of there. Get up. Get up and walk around."

He never thought that she had no money, no way to "get out of there." He couldn't understand why she couldn't leave her house, the quiet and the mountains. In the end, of course, she did. Humiliated, she begged for money and allowed him to rent her the apartment on the channel. Three days a week, she drove through snarled traffic to appointments, terrified that she might hit another car.

The rest of her days she spent sleeping or trying to make the small apartment hold her. She kept her shutters closed against the sounds of squealing tires, blaring music, couples arriving home after dark, their sharp footsteps and laughter ringing in the night. "I can't live here," she thought. "I will not thrive."

Failure to thrive, a term for war orphans who never gain weight or grow. She'd known of solitary pigs that wouldn't gain and horses turned out into empty pastures where they paced for weeks along the fence. She found herself avoiding daylight, waiting for dusk before she ventured onto the patio. When darkness pooled around her feet, she thought of wharf rats. She hung her heels on the rung of her chair but went on sitting, watching for the tiny running lights of boats returning from the sea.

Her father called, demanding to know why she wasn't happy, as if her state of mind reflected on him and his generosity. Even if she tried to tell him, he would never understand how the apartment felt like nothing, a bubble floating in the air. She couldn't get any *purchase* here, no traction.

"I'm trying," she said, but was aware that she'd been in the apartment for a month and never walked the few blocks to the beach, never waded in the surf. She kept telling herself that anyone would love to live where she lived, the winter sun glancing off blue water and the white sails floating past, shining like a boy's dream of toy boats.

She let the bulb in the patio lamp burn out and found she could sit by the hours in darkness, wondering why large yachts would motor out in the night. "Where could they be going?" She heard pelicans dive, the flat impact and splash. Late in the night, almost early morning, she heard a sound like human breathing. She thought of channel swimmers turning their capped heads for air or illegal aliens silently making for shore. But she couldn't imagine how she could hear such a small sound so clearly. On a different night, when she heard it again, she forced herself to cross the asphalt path and peer into the water. A wave furled sideways into the rock and sighed in its retreat.

She kept her vigil on the channel. One night she heard a scuffling in the leaves and looked down. In the pale light, an opossum wandered slowly forward, his nose lifted as if he were navigating blind. She watched him stop and tilt his head, looking vague and innocent. When he came too close, she whispered, "No, you don't want to come up here." And the soft gray body stopped. The opossum listened. Then very slowly he reversed direction and drifted back into the dark.

"Wharf rats," she thought, missing for the first time the skunks and deer, the foxes and coyotes that wandered through the ranch at night. "I'm not going to die," she thought, "but I may never go home." In the emergency room, they had told her to wait despite the blood that dripped down the backs of her hands and onto the floor. When her vision began to close in like the shutter of a broken camera, a nurse in white grasped her shoulder and pushed her into a wheelchair.

She never saw the doctor. The cowl of darkness and tears occluded her vision, making her aware only of his voice as he pierced the skin of her inner arm with a needle and thread. She cried and thrashed until an orderly restrained her. She cried like a child, begging the doctor to stop. "It hurts. It hurts too much."

He ignored her, speaking only to the aide beside him, his words compressed with anger. "She should have thought of that before."

"I'm sorry," she said. "I'm so sorry." Crying, she repeated these words through forty-seven stitches, sorry for causing this man so much trouble. It seemed right that a man intent on saving lives would be so furious with her.

It was nearly a week later before she heard it again, the splash to the surface and the quick release of air. The sound was so intimate, she wondered if she was really hearing it, until it came again. She pictured spies approaching, and for the first time since childhood, she thought of frogmen.

Her father would understand solitary confinement, war prisoners trapped in the dark. Why couldn't he understand how easy it was to get lost? How, by the time you try to kill yourself, you aren't yourself anymore? She began to understand her father's anger, the contempt that separates the living from the dead. The doctor's fury had not been caused by her.

Months seemed to pass as if they were days. In June, fog banks moved in from the ocean, and every afternoon, the channel drifted in and out of mist until it disappeared. She could hear distant horns and hardware clanking on the masts of boats she couldn't see. By the time the sun burned through, it had traveled west in the sky and left her patio shadowed and cold, but on the far side of the path, the light still warmed the asphalt and glanced off the white boats and water beyond.

She thought, "I could just walk into the sun, as if I were walking from winter to spring," and with the channel on her left, she began to make her way toward the ocean. The sun glared directly in her eyes, blacking out her vision. When she stopped to unfold her sunglasses, she heard the sound again—the breach for air, the expulsion of breath. She stepped into the grass and weeds beside the path and peered over the rocks. The tide was high, but she saw nothing but blue water.

A black speck appeared far away near the center of the channel, a duck or pelican bobbing to the surface. She looked again, and it emerged as a head shoveling through the water like the head of a swimming dog. It disappeared and was followed by a slick, dark curve of body.

From so far away, the sound was just the same, just as intimate. The sea lion raised his head and expelled air before he dove again. She watched the glistening animal dive and surface, swimming underwater for great lengths, then surfacing again. He rolled over and circled a buoy, swimming so near she could see his round eyes and his whiskers before he reversed direction and disappeared.

She thought about sailors too long at sea lured into the rocks by sirens. How they would have heard the wind sing in their rigging and the sound, so close, of human breath. But only one boat broke the surface of the channel, sending behind it a long, narrow wave, a twisted, pale-green ribbon. In the wave, she could see the sea lion swimming, his entire body curving up and down, a motion like a deft hand sewing perfect stitches in a baby blanket.

In the next weeks, when the sun stayed overhead all day, she was drawn to the warm bands of light the color of clarified butter. To be in the sun as long as she could, she began to wake when it rose in the morning. She watched, and on rare days, she saw the glistening sea lion. Sitting outside at night, she heard him approach in the darkness, the sound of his breath as close as her own.

TURTLE

As a wedding gift, a grown niece presented them with a turtle. A saucer-sized, red-eared slider. They slipped it into the small pond in their new patio, where it promptly disappeared beneath a jungle of lily pads and water hyacinths, safe from the neighborhood cats. They fed it hamburger. On sunny days, it made an awkward climb up onto the surrounding rocks and basked. That was how she noticed something protruding from beneath its tiny tail, a growth of some kind, preventing the turtle from withdrawing entirely into its shell.

"If it can't retract," she told her husband, "the cats will get it."

Together, they studied the turtle from a distance, bending for closer looks. They couldn't tell what it was that hung beneath the turtle's tail.

"Let's just keep an eye on it," her husband said.

They might have done something had they known what to do. Did veterinarians *treat* turtles?

She phoned the niece, who confessed that the turtle had cost only seven dollars in the first place.

"Still," she said, "you need a specialist, an expert in exotic pets."

"Exotic pets?"

"Snakes and reptiles. Birds."

"For a *seven-dollar* turtle?"

"Check the phone book."

The yellow pages yielded only one veterinarian who specialized in "exotics," but his office, miraculously, was on the main street of their suburban town. Again, she consulted her husband.

"I have to go to the bank after work, " he said. "We might as well call and ask if he can see us."

. . .

She netted the turtle and placed it in a cardboard liquor box with grass and paper for a bed. Her husband carried it into the vet's office and stayed until she and the box were settled.

"Nothing exotic about the waiting room," she thought. She sat alone on a beige chair in a beige room no more than twelve feet square. No receptionist had greeted her. She waited for the doctor's door to open.

Instead, two women entered from the street door, an older one, obviously the mother, and a tall, homely younger one. The older woman settled herself in a chair and said hello. The younger remained standing, a very large, red and iridescent-green rooster trapped under her arm. While the older woman began to chat, the younger stalked about the small room, saying nothing.

"What have you got in the box?" the mother wished to know.

"A turtle."

"What's wrong with it?"

"We don't know. There's a protuberance under his tail. We don't know what it is."

"Oh," the woman said, "my daughter will know." She caught the younger woman's attention and nodded. "Take a look."

The woman holding the rooster sidled over and glanced down in the box. She studied the contents for a brief moment.

"It's a turd," she pronounced with terse authority.

With no further comment, she returned to stand, aloof and detached, beside her mother. The rooster blinked a yellow, predatory eye.

When the door to the inner sanctum opened, she left the two women and carried the box into a second room, not an examining room, but a kind of office. The veterinarian, a narrow man with thick glasses, lifted the turtle from the box, held it up to the light, and examined its rear.

Prolapsed rectum was the diagnosis. She listened to the prognosis, and the projected expense. Forty dollars for examining the turtle in the first place. Another forty for the operation. And *another* forty to put the turtle to sleep if they decided against the surgery.

"I don't know," she said. "My husband's gone to the bank. I had better wait and see what he thinks."

She returned to the waiting room and waited, the turtle quiet in his box. They were newly married, both of them working. They had just bought a house in an older, gracious suburb. They couldn't afford to spend eighty dollars on a turtle. She waited and worried.

Her husband would never authorize this. She knew him. He kept careful accounts of every penny they earned, every dollar they spent. They had both had reckless, alcoholic parents, and she had married him partly for his courage, partly for his caution.

When her husband finally returned, she stood to deliver the bad news.

"It's only a seven-dollar turtle," she said.

To her great surprise, he blinked and his eyes took on a liquid shine.

"Do it," he said.

"Do it?"

"Let's do the operation."

The doctor carried the turtle and his box away, and they drove home. This was Friday. They were to telephone the next morning. When they called, the doctor informed them that he wished to hold the turtle for "observation." They should call again on Monday.

On weekends, they took their morning coffee on the patio. Because they were saving for outdoor furniture, they sat on the steps and gazed at the pond. It seemed curiously empty, incomplete. They worried about the turtle.

On Monday, they phoned again and were told by the doctor—there were complications. "Complications?" they thought. When the doctor said he wished to keep the turtle one more day, they began to grow suspicious.

"Died under the knife," she said. "He's out looking for *another* turtle."

"Or he never planned to operate at all," her husband said. "He just went out and bought another turtle." They laughed until they couldn't stand. They pictured the doctor—"keeping the turtle under observation." It would be like watching rocks.

It wasn't until Wednesday that the doctor called. The prognosis was good. Five days and eighty dollars later, a turtle was restored to them. A turtle that might, or might not, be their turtle. The protuberance was gone, and the turtle was returned to the pond—safe from cats and predators.

"At least he didn't charge us room and board," her husband said.

After dinner, they carried their coffee out to the patio and sat on the steps. The air was balmy, a cool blessing after the hot day. The turtle lifted his head from the water, showing the blood-red stripes along his neck, looking for food. They were filled with the amber glow that parents sometimes feel, the momentary, fragile joy of making a safe place.

"You told me you never wanted pets," she said. Her husband grinned with an embarrassment, a shyness she had never seen. He raised his chin and tried to frown.

"He's not a pet," he said. "Now he's an investment."

URSUS HORRIBILIS

A man had been killed in a campground by a grizzly bear; the announcement came over the TV from a blond park ranger with a flat, midwestern voice. She seemed unconcerned. Yes, they would release the name of the victim once the family had been found. Yes, the bear would be destroyed.

"How will they know they have the *right* bear?" I asked my stepfather.

"Track 'em. Hell, all those bears have collars on 'em

anyhow. They'll just raise him on the radio—ask him what he had for lunch."

"Oh *stop*," I said.

When we first moved to Wyoming, my mother worked as a cook at a different hunting camp each fall. Some hunter had told me about a bear that tore apart a tent and ate the people in their sleeping bags, and after that, I had terrible nightmares.

When she wasn't hauling food and water or cooking, my mother used to read. That's why she liked these jobs. She read that the Indians were never attacked by grizzly bears. "The bears feed on fruit and bugs and carrion," she said. "They don't eat people." In the daytime, I used to ponder how many *bugs* it would take to feed a grizzly bear, but at night, I couldn't sleep until my mother crawled into her sleeping bag beside me.

They interviewed the same blonde woman on the news the next night. "There is some evidence," she said, "that the victim was deceased at the time of the attack."

"A suicide?" the newsman asked.

"We are not sure of the cause of death," the ranger said, "but the search for the bear will continue."

I couldn't believe it. I looked at my mother and stepfather.

"They're going to shoot the bear."

"That's what they do," my mother said.

"But he didn't kill anybody," I said. "The man was *already* dead."

"He'll go after someone else," my stepdad said.

"Who?" I asked. "The *next* dead camper?"

I felt tears coming, and I was angry with my mother. Why didn't she speak up for the bear?

When we used to go to the hunting camps, my mother took me out of school and taught me math herself. I was good at all the other subjects, English and science and French, and I didn't have much trouble keeping up. After lunch, when the men were resting, we hiked to a shady place where we could dangle our feet in a creek or see a long way across a meadow. That's where I learned long division and how to multiply fractions. That's where, when I was twelve, I started my first period.

I was surprised that my mother had brought along supplies, and I hated the bulge of the pad in my jeans. I was sure everyone could see, and I was terrified something would leak.

That first night, it hurt so much, I began to cry. I kept thinking of the story where the bear attacked the campers in their tent. It was because one of them was a woman who was having her period. My mother cried, too, for her own reasons I think now. Finally, she shook me by the arm and said, "What are *you* crying about? You have your *mother* with you." She sounded so pathetic, we both started to laugh.

My mother is a beauty, and I had never understood why my real dad had left her before I was born. The men in the hunting camps watched her. I watched them. They were almost always city men with money who only cared about "bagging" an elk. I avoided the place where the gutted elk hung from crossbars lashed between trees, far enough away from the tents to keep bears and coyotes away. But there was always that smell of blood, a sharp, foreign smell, like tarnished silver.

The next summer, my mother left me with my best friend's family and worked on a boat in Alaska. "You're too old," she said, "for hunting camp."

I wrote her a letter a day about working as a cabin girl on a dude ranch. All summer, while my mother was out fishing, my friend Janet and I were locked inside some tiny cabin changing sheets or in the kitchen washing piles of dirty plates.

That's when the longing started. Janet was my age, but so much older in her ways. Her boyfriend worked on a ranch in Montana, and we used to lie on the freshly made beds and talk about him. When people are in love, I learned, it's almost as good to *talk* about the person as to be with him. I made up crushes on boys who came to the ranch, not to feel quite so left out. I described the boys to my mother so often, I began to believe my own lies.

My mother flew home early when the boat she worked on sank. I made her tell me about it over and over, how the storm came up and the coast guard had to get them all off of the boat. But she came home with money. We bought a little house in town, and my mother went to work at a fancy restaurant. My stepfather owned it.

When the man was attacked by the bear, I was home because I was taking a year off from college, though I didn't know yet if they would take me back. I had fallen in love the first week of school—with a janitor. He was also a musician who played bass guitar in a band on the weekends. He stood up on the stage, barely moving, his long fingers draped over the strings, holding the whole band together. I couldn't believe it when he sat down next to me at the break. I tried to keep up with my courses, but spending so much time with Cal, I missed out on too much. I went to my classes and sat through labs and lectures, but I couldn't keep my mind on things. I couldn't make any friends in the dorm. The other students seemed so young to me. When Cal finally told me he had a wife, it was too late. I was thin and sick and on probation.

But I was a star at the restaurant. As it had in many resort towns, real estate had gotten so expensive that workers couldn't live there anymore. They were bussing people in from Idaho, and college kids were camped out in the forest.

We had a ritual. After the restaurant closed, we walked home and watched the late news. My mother brewed a cup of tea, and my stepfather mixed himself a cocktail. Some nights he offered me a beer, as if it were a rite of passage, a big deal, but mostly I just sat with them a little while before

I went to bed. Working in a restaurant leaves you exhausted but excited at the same time. It's hard to fall asleep.

The next time they interviewed the blonde ranger, she gave the name of the dead man, and a blurred photo came on the screen. My mother sat up and listened. It appeared he was a homeless man who'd gone up to the campground just to sleep.

"I knew him," my mother said.

My stepfather was surprised. "How could you know him?"

"He came to the kitchen," she said. "He wanted food."

"What did you give him, rack of lamb? Beef in brandy sauce?" He was naming my mother's specialties.

"I didn't give him anything . . ." my mother said. "I don't know why."

"Well, we can't feed every bum that comes around."

The next night my mother went straight to bed when we got home.

When we were at hunting camp, I told my mother the dreams about bears. I would be skiing in the dreams—in the summer, without skis—sailing down a mountain, when I'd see at the bottom a huge bear and two cubs. Sometimes, one of the cubs was white. But I always saw them too late and had to crash through trees and branches to get past. I barely escaped, and then I remembered, my mother was just behind me. I stopped and tried to go back, but the invisible skis wouldn't go uphill. I always woke up full of fear and dread.

My mother told me how bears are born in the den and are tiny, as tiny as newborn puppies. "They're like little lumps of dough," my mother said. "People used to think the mother bear *licked* them into shape.

"Bears are shy," she told me, "and there aren't many left. If you were to see one in real life, you would feel very fortunate. Start looking every day, and you'll understand how safe you are. I'd love to see one," she said, smiling at me, "from a distance."

Later, she did. After she came back from Alaska, she told me a story about a blond bear in a national park where bears had never been hunted. They'd never fed from garbage dumps or been shot with tranquilizer guns—with PCP— and moved to other locations. She told me this story in a quiet voice full of awe.

"The rangers tell you not to approach the bears, just to look from a distance. I walked out toward the beach and sat down on a rock, a large, flat rock. At first, I didn't see the bear. She was tossing seaweed around near the water. I watched her for a long time, thinking she couldn't see me. But suddenly, she lifted up and started loping right toward me. I froze. She stopped so close, I could smell her. She was huffing. The rangers said that was a sign the bear was stressed. They told us not to look them in the eye. So I looked down. The bear was huffing, but I don't think I was even breathing. Then, I don't know why, I just had to do it, I looked up. I truly thought I was going to die. But the bear looked at me, just for a second, and turned away. I sat on the rock and watched her lumber away, then I stayed right there, maybe an hour more."

"What did it feel like," I asked my mother, "when you looked at the bear?"

"It was like looking into the eyes of a strange dog—or your own dog—and knowing it might bite you. When I did it, I knew I didn't understand anything. There is a whole world we don't know a thing about. After the bear was gone, then it was like skiing without skis, like your dreams—

where you can skim over the earth without effort, you can go anywhere. . . ."

I waited for a time when I would be alone with my mother. We didn't talk anymore, not the way we used to, and I couldn't think of a way to bring up the subject, but finally, my stepfather sent us home early. We had a table of twelve lingering over some celebration, an engagement party I think. He said he'd stay and close up.

I realized how long it had been since I'd been alone with my mother. We stood in the kitchen waiting for the kettle to boil.

"Why didn't you give that man some food?" I asked her.

"I don't know," my mother said. "I usually do . . . give them food."

"Them who?"

"We get a lot of transients now," my mother said. "They come to the kitchen door, or I see them going through the garbage." She poured boiling water into the cups. "I just started thinking—I do it out of guilt. We have so much . . . sometimes I want to give it all away.

"He was smart, that man. Filthy, but smart. He had very

bright, blue eyes. He looked old, but he wasn't. He had those clear blue eyes.

"Just that one night—I felt guilty for feeling guilty. I just said 'no.'"

For the first time in so long, I put my arm around her shoulders. I couldn't remember my stepfather touching her. I couldn't remember the last time anybody touched *me*. I missed it, and I thought my mother must miss it, too. When I squeezed her into my chest, her ribs seemed to fold into themselves as if they were on hinges. After I let go, the warmth of her body stayed with me.

"Sometimes," my mother said, "I wish we were back at hunting camp. Everything was so simple then. It was just the two of us."

"And the bears," I said.

My mother managed a smile.

"And the bears," she agreed.

VULTURE

On the day his lover died, a family he had never met before arrived to ship the body home. Later that same afternoon, he flew to Mexico. It was in Baja that he first saw vultures perched on ragged fences, as if their hunched and lurking silhouettes were comic advertisements for the point of no return. On the long, hot bus trip from the airport, he saw miles of dusty desert. From time to time, a house appeared, a blue or pink or yellow cement-block house, overgrown with lavish bougainvillea. A plump woman seated next to him kept repeating, "Oh, wait until you get there. It's not like this at all. It's *nice* in Cabo." He suspected the people in those houses were proud of them. He wouldn't mind, he thought, moving into one right then just to get out of the heat.

The woman explained to the couple opposite how to locate the "real" market, the vegetable market. "The fruit is marvelous," she announced before her face grew heavy with past betrayal, "but watch out for the papayas. They look all right until you get them home—but then they turn on you like that." She snapped her plump fingers. He watched the eyes of the couple glisten with restrained laughter. "Watch out for the papayas," he repeated to himself, "they'll turn on you."

He slept in the hotel the rest of the day—in a *casita* with a thatched roof and no glass in the windows. He dreamed, as he had before, that he was a young soldier on leave, running on the grass, who awoke to the permanent truth that his leg was gone. He wept in protest: Running should be life; the truth should be the nightmare. In his dreams, sorrow loomed, a black Gibraltar shape that filled him from within. This time though, the dream faded with the light of day. He felt an ease in the body he hadn't felt all winter, the pleasure of walking to the shower naked and emerging in his bathing suit. Later in the morning, he walked along the beach. The blue Pacific stretched away to the far, hazy distance, and he felt like Balboa, discovering *an ocean*. He noticed, for the first time in years, all the tiny bones and muscles in his feet, how they splayed and curled to hold him upright as he waded in the shallow waves. His feet were so large and pale they gleamed like fish bellies under the water.

He noticed the smell—the smell of Mexican beaches: salt and sea air, mixed with diesel fumes and sewage. He cringed each time a boat or Jet Ski roared into the shallow water, barely skirting the dark heads of children bobbing in the surf. He spent an evening at a dusky nightclub, just opened by a rock star, watching for celebrities who never appeared. He walked into town on the rough concrete of cracked and broken sidewalks and went on walking, out into the blazing heat of treeless blocks of concrete houses and bodegas, where, unbelievably, the few people on the street greeted him in Spanish as he passed.

He thought of going out to sea on a charter boat and went so far as to step inside a small, dirty office to inquire. The walls were hung with fly-specked photographs, so old the blue had washed away to yellow, of men standing as straight as the enormous fish hanging beside them.

The fishing boat chugged out past the smaller boats, the Jet Skis, and the sparkling cruise ships into a white, blinding glare off the ocean. The chop of the waves and the smell of diesel smoke made his head ache and his stomach pitch. Two young Mexicans, their skin nearly black from the sun, served him beer from a cooler and showed him how to sit in the anchored chair, but it was hours before the spotter found a fish. Three men, himself and two others, were strapped into their chairs. They braced their feet while the boatmen baited their hooks and demonstrated how to trail them in the water.

When the fish struck, he was sure he'd snagged his line on an anchor, a deep-sea wreck. The grab nearly pulled his arms out of the sockets. The other men cheered and watched the water, waiting for the fish to rise. It arced out of the ocean, gleaming like something not from this earth—a siren glistening with gems. He fought the fish. The other men offered to relieve him, but he hardly heard what they were saying. His muscles quivered and burned, but he leaned into the pain as if the pain itself could hold him, like a wall of stone. He rested, like a weightlifter between the clean and jerk, no longer wishing for the days that should have been.

When he gave the slightest nod, a signal prearranged, the sun-blackened Mexican boy stepped in close. He flashed a lethal silver blade and cut the line.

WATCH DOG

Not for the first time, the older children urged their little sister, dressed in tired pink tulle, toward their mother.

"Santa Claus can't find me here," the child said, grabbing a fistful of her mother's skirt.

Lifting her cocktail to keep it from spilling, their mother untangled the grubby hand without looking down.

"We want to go home," the children wheedled.

In the midst of conversation, their mother seemed hardly to see them.

"Then go on," she said. "I'll be there soon."

"Can't," the boy said. "Sissy won't go past the dogs."

"Hold her hand."

"She won't *go*."

"Sissy?" Their mother's perfume drifted to them as she turned and bent to talk to the child. "I think Santa's been to our house. You better go and see."

Released, the children ran from one apartment building in a complex of plain military housing to another and climbed a set of cement stairs painted white. Near their own floor, they heard the frantic scrambling of toenails on wood flooring, and an impact, as if the dogs had thrown their weight against the door. The little girl refused to budge.

A retired colonel and his wife had taken the apartment across the hall for the winter, moving in with two sleek black and tan Dobermans. The children had observed the gray-haired man in a plaid driving cap as he worked the dogs in a quadrangle between the stucco buildings. They had watched the dogs circle widely with their muzzles to the ground but their ears straight up, and return instantly when he blew into a silent whistle.

But the little girl was terrified by the noise and would not pass the door until her older sister picked her up and placed her scuffed pink ballet slippers on top of her own party shoes, the way a father might do to teach a little girl to dance. "Close your eyes," she said.

Sissy held her arms stiff at her sides and squeezed her eyes shut. Her sister wrapped her arms around her, and they walked double past the door. Her brother led the way into their own apartment, and they saw right away the blinking lights of the Christmas tree. While they had been at the party, someone had delivered presents. They sat down promptly, suddenly wide awake with excitement. The boy distributed the packages, and without hesitation, they tore away the wrapping paper. Inside the boxes, they found new socks and underwear. The older girl unwrapped a Girl Scout uniform and a green felt beret. An aunt had mailed them a coffee can full of homemade cookies, a dozen different kinds, each one folded in its own square of waxed paper. There were no toys.

They sat vacant-eyed before the tree, not speaking. As young as they were, they knew their mother had done something terribly wrong. She was the only divorced woman on the military base, and they were reminded daily at school, that this, and being poor, were shameful. People treated them as if they were bad, dirty somehow or up to no good.

Without washing or brushing their teeth, the children removed their party clothes and put themselves to bed. The older children lay awake, waiting for their mother. When she didn't come, they felt a dead, dark boredom, as if they had been shut up in black boxes where the walls were slowly closing in. During the night, they woke to the frantic barking of the dogs and drifted back to sleep again.

In the morning, they left their mother snoring lightly in her bed and ran outdoors into clear, cold sunshine. They wanted to find out what their friends had gotten for Christmas. Across the quadrangle, they saw the colonel and his wife and the two dogs returning from a walk along the curve of the blue bay. When the couple stopped to rest, the children approached.

"Sissy's scared of your dogs," the older girl said. "I'm not. I'm not afraid of dogs."

The woman ran her hand down the sleek neck of the dog closest to her. "You don't have to be afraid of these dogs," she said. She knelt and looked directly at Sissy, who stood just behind her sister's knee, worrying her lower lip.

"These are war dogs," she said. "Retired." She pointed as she introduced them: "Kurt and Schatzi."

The husband said, "They're named after famous dogs that went to war."

"Our dad went to the war," Sissy said.

"So did Kurt and Schatzi," he answered, and lifted his hand. Instantly, the dogs froze, on full alert. He raised his fingers and both dogs crouched low. When his palm tipped, they began to crawl, inching along the grass with their ears flat to their heads.

He released them with a silent whistle, and they returned to stand beside him and his wife. Sissy smiled. Her sister pushed her gently forward. Slowly, she advanced on the male dog, her small, dirty palm held flat. The man nodded, and the dog stepped forward and sniffed. When he sat back on his haunches and lifted a paw, Sissy squealed and looked back at her sister.

"Go ahead," she said.

The dog's paw was as big as Sissy's hand, so she grasped the side of it and shook while Kurt tipped his head and seemed to raise his eyebrows. Then she stepped back and gave the dog a smart salute. Everybody laughed, and Sissy looked confused.

"Don't be afraid of these dogs," the neighbor said.

"Did they kill Japs?" The boy spoke for the first time.

"Oh no," the man said. "We sent them ahead to sniff out land mines. A dog can smell an enemy soldier no matter where he's hiding. He can even hear the wind pass over the wire of a booby trap. The K-9 corps saved the lives of our soldiers."

The children ran home and pounded up the stairs. Inside the apartment, their mother sat drinking coffee, a cigarette held low in her hand.

"What did Santa bring you?" she asked.

"Socks," they said.

"That's all?"

They looked at her, puzzled.

"Go look again," she said.

Far back against the wall, under the tree, they saw three packages they hadn't seen the night before, large, square boxes wrapped in red and green and blue foil. The packages had no ribbons. Instead, their names had been written across the fronts with glue and silver glitter.

They opened the presents carefully to save the shining paper, and inside each box, they found a pair of roller skates.

Outside in minutes, they sat awkwardly on the sidewalk to fit their shoes into the skates and tighten them down with keys. One by one, they were up and skating, bending forward at the waist, alert to every seam and crack in the concrete. The older girl towed Sissy by the hand.

Their mother had told them the presents came from the neighbors across the hall. Though the cards had read "From Kurt and Schatzi," the children never remembered thanking them. But they never forgot the glittering boxes, or how it felt to fly along the rough sidewalk, their shirts and pant legs ballooning with air, their sweaty foreheads cooled by the breeze that swept across the chop of the blue bay.

X :
THE UNKNOWN
QUANTITY

In the morning, there is a live wire fallen down across our driveway, lolling like a round, black jump rope, a walker's tightwire, swinging two feet off the ground. The far end attaches still to a leaning utility pole, gray with age and pitted with holes. The other end, amazingly, remains connected to the corner of the house. A light wind barely shifts the weight of it, and sparks sizzle at the pole.

I think about safety films I've seen. What action to take in a gale, in an electrical storm. But there has been no storm, no rain, no lightning. And I can't remember whether one should stay in the car or run. Can the tires, no longer made of rubber, save you?

I call in the dogs, and though we seldom have a visitor, I wonder if I should post a warning sign at the end of the drive. I call the electric company, but no one is in the office, and it takes several calls to reach a woman at home. She promises that her husband will bring a bucket truck "sometime today."

My own husband is working in Baggs, Wyoming, conducting an agricultural survey for the government. Every year, they mail forms, pages of questions, to every landowner in the U.S., asking, "How many acres are planted in hay, in corn, in oats? . . ." "How many head of livestock do you feed? . . ." In the corner of the west where my husband works, there's always some old-timer who refuses to answer the survey, and the government actually sends out a roving team of housewives and cash-poor ranchers to find out why.

Though we have lived here only a few months, my husband turns out to be very good at this job. He has a graduate degree in political science but has taken to the west as if he were a native. He can sit in the coffee shop for hours without saying one word. He begins his sentences with, "If a fella wanted to, how would a fella go about . . ." He has a natural gift for never asking a direct question, and I picture him sitting for hours around kitchen tables, coaxing information out of ranchers who in point of fact simply *hate* the government.

I am from the city, from the suburbs, sunny places where it never even snows, and it makes sense to me to call the electric company when a live electric wire is hanging where anyone could walk or drive right into it. I'm still unpacking boxes from the move, scrubbing hand-sawn and many-times-painted cupboards in our plain, asbestos-shingled ranch house. From time to time, I venture out and stare at the wire, keeping my distance as if it were a thick, black snake. I wonder if I should call again.

The weather, though not storming, is bleak. It is November, and the hay fields that were golden stubble when we arrived are fading, large patches dampened to a lichen gray. The sky is blue, but so distant, the land seems abandoned. I feel exposed, waiting in the treeless yard.

Finally, a white truck with black lettering on the door and two heavy men in hard hats in the cab pulls into the driveway. I can see a folded hydraulic bucket in the back of the truck and go out to stand on the steps. It is so cold, my nose begins to run, and I have to go back inside for a tissue. When I return, one of the men has buckled cleats to his round-toed boots and climbed the rotting pole, which threatens to give under his weight. He descends the pole without touching anything and walks across the driveway, looking down, to me.

"It ain't our deal," he says.

"What?"

"Not our pole," he tells me.

I still don't understand. If it's not their pole, whose is it?

"I'm sorry ma'am," he says. "We didn't set that pole. I can't touch it."

It still takes me a while to understand that some previous owner owned the pole—and now we own it, and I'm supposed to somehow fix the wire myself.

The man is walking back to his truck. I have to trot after him.

"But the wire's live? Right? Isn't it?" I'm circling as far away from the wire as I can get and still be able to make him hear me. I realize, I'm terrified of the wire. I'm terrified of electricity. "Isn't it dangerous?"

The two men stand beside their truck conferring. The older, his hair slicked back with some kind of oil, looks like the comic villain in a melodrama. The younger, his hands and overalls actually black with soot or grease, reaches into the cab of the truck for a microphone and speaks into the radio.

"We're out here at the White Bridge. Lady's got a problem."

I have some trouble hearing myself spoken of as "ma'am" and "lady," as if I were older than I am, doddering. I think of myself as young, as strong. I've moved to Wyoming to live on a ranch. And I'm getting ready to beg this man to fix my wire.

And I do. "Please," I say to him. "I understand it's not your deal. But my husband isn't home. He's working. He won't be back until Saturday. That's a live wire, right? Please. Isn't there something you can do?"

As I'm speaking I realize I've done the unforgivable. I've put someone in a position where he might have to say "No."

I haven't said, "Well, if a woman wanted to, how would a woman go about getting someone to raise that goddamned killer wire off her driveway?"

"Well, I don't know . . ." he says.

"Please," I say, and now, genuinely, I am crying.

I retreat to the porch—a good, safe distance—while the older man backs up the truck and the younger man ascends in the hydraulic bucket. Enormous clippers and pliers hang from his leather belt. The afternoon has grown so cold I am shivering. I look over to the fallow field behind me just as a blanket of wild ducks takes flight. The same dark color as the earth, they fill the horizon with tiny x's, as if great handfuls of cloves have been tossed to the sky. The week we moved in, my husband drove me to the best sporting-goods store in Jackson, Wyoming, during the off-season sales, and bought me Sorrell pack boots and a two-hundred-dollar down jacket. But I don't have them on. In the hills surrounding the ranch, I can still see yellow, the leaves on aspen trees, which are brighter and more yellow against the blue November sky.

This is something van Gogh knew. What happens when blue and yellow stand next to each other. The blue in the sky, and the ochre on the ground. There is an emptiness between we can't explain, a hollow in the universe.

Standing on the porch, I can almost smell it on the air, that vast blue space, from which winter is coming.

YELLOW JACKET

Never underestimate the capacity of children to endure misery. They can develop the dull patience of long-term prisoners. They are in love with people who constantly leave them behind to work or travel or even sleep. The small lovers agonize in their absence because they don't know where their parents have gone, for how long, or for what reason.

Melissa was such a child. She would remember all her life being left in a nursery, sitting alone in a playpen. She would recall the sweet-sour smell of plastic toys, of white bread and canned soup. The endless waiting.

A dark-haired, solemn child of no particular beauty, she begged to stay home from school and from camp. But her parents insisted that it was good for her to play with other children. School for her was agony—simply because she couldn't play ball. She was never chosen for a team, and during recess, she exhausted the time circling the trunks of ancient oak trees, jumping from one raised and gnarled root to another, her palm scratching along the bark. She learned to pretend interest and occupation.

She learned to read minds. She knew her parents fought in the night after her bedtime. She knew they fought about money, about her father leaving on so many trips so his boss wouldn't fire him. She knew her teacher didn't like her, that he thought she was judging him in her solemnity, that he thought she was bad. She knew the other children were perplexed; she made them feel guilty, the way a person in a wheelchair could make her feel sorry and afraid at the same time.

She began to practice in the park, delaying on her way home from school. She sat on a bench and watched the nannies with strollers, men in suits with folded newspapers, joggers, and the homeless men. Each day when she sat down and placed her satchel on the seat beside her, she saw a gray overcoat curled on the bench across the asphalt path, a man with matted blond hair and heavy boots. If a breeze came up, she caught his smell, a smell of garbage left out on the street too long and, unexpectedly, of gasoline.

He never made a sound, but she began to hear him dreaming.

He spoke as if to aliens, people watching him from high above. He kept telling them his exact location, mimicking a kind of radio, with static sounds between the words.

"I'm here . . . two clicks from a big gray building, squawk, they can't get me here . . . squawk . . . blue tree, two o'clock . . ."

She thought of moving to a different bench—or waking him up. But both thoughts frightened her. She was only safe right there, on her bench. She practiced, and she managed to make his voice so small she barely heard it, but she went looking and found the big gray building, and the tree.

She made her parents' voices small, her teacher's, and the people in the next apartment. Yet, she still knew when her father was fired. Her mother wanted a divorce, but neither of them moved out. They both went to work every day as they always had. But they were suddenly much nicer.

They began to plan her birthday party, inviting the children of the people from their offices and children from the building. Melissa would have tried to stop the plan, but she couldn't have said how she knew about the big surprise. Her dad suggested walks in the park after supper. They walked right past her bench, and she knew what the people were saying to themselves.

"Must be her dad," they thought. "Handsome man. And so young. Too bad she doesn't look like him. Or maybe she does. Looks better on a man."

On these evenings, the homeless man was never on his bench, and she wondered where he went at night. It came to her, his protectors wouldn't be able to find him at night, no matter how careful his directions. He would be hiding somewhere safe.

On the day of the party, her mother dressed up in a silk dress the color of geraniums, and her dad wore a white shirt and loafers. They both looked so clean. Her mother insisted that Melissa wear a stiff, itchy dress with a skirt that stuck out. It was too young for her, but she let her mother button all the tiny buttons up the back. Even before they left the house, the stiff trim at the armholes began to scratch into her flesh.

They told her they would be walking through the park to Tavern on the Green for a birthday brunch. They crossed the avenue together, three abreast, her mother holding her hand. Once inside the park, it seemed to her that everyone was talking at once. She never came to the park on Sunday. The paths were crowded with people: kids on bicycles and Rollerblades, walkers and runners and old people strolling. Their voices came at her like passing trains, one louder than another.

"Keep up," her mother said.

She forced her legs to move faster, and struggled to keep the voices small. She focused on her father, on what was in his mind.

"Just get me through this day," he thought. "Please God, just get me through this one last day."

For the first time, she felt sorry for him. Her new shoes pinched her feet, but she struggled to keep up. She took his hand.

The caterer had arranged white-covered tables on the slope, just above the place where she sat on her bench. The sun, by then, was hot, and the food on the tables, even under their umbrellas, looked tired. Everyone stood up and shouted, "Surprise!" and the waiters began to pour punch into stemmed plastic glasses.

Melissa worried about the money. How could her parents afford this? The children were served miniature hot dogs and hamburgers, with tiny bottles of ketchup and mustard. The parents had crêpes, like blintzes, with bowls of sour cream and jam. She was shown to a seat at the head of the largest table and served a plate. Her mother, pleased with herself and looking almost gay, gave a nod toward Melissa. The guests couldn't eat until she picked up her fork, she knew that.

She lifted her fork and looked out over the table. The children had all come with their parents, and the parents began to talk and laugh. The children in their fancy clothes, white shirts and frilly dresses, squirted ketchup on their plates. One entire table had been covered with a pyramid of gifts wrapped in colored papers, and a pretend bar was set up to the side.

When she heard the voice, the squawk and static of the radio, she looked over toward her bench. The homeless man sat up, his face nearly gray and his eyes not quite open. He took both hands and rubbed hard at his face, as if to scrub the sleep off.

She looked down at her plate. Her hamburgers and hot dogs were swarming with bees, tiny yellow bees. She stood up and accidentally knocked her chair down. The bees seemed to hover all around her. The parents and children backed away from the tables, waving their hands vaguely in front of their faces. Some were trying to laugh. One of the children began to cry in rough, hiccuping cries.

Her mother conferred rapidly with the caterers. They nodded, and one jogged over to the bar and returned with a can of insect spray.

Her mother became more alarmed.

"You can't spray the food . . ."

She turned her head and stopped still, all the pink drained from her face.

Melissa followed where her mother looked. The homeless man was close, lumbering toward them. Her mother made a move, as if to snatch her from harm, but Melissa stepped toward the man. His thoughts were unreadable, but she wasn't afraid.

He walked to her table, and though his hands were large and black with grime, he lifted the spoon from the jam with great delicacy. He placed a dollop on the end of his first finger and held it out to the bees.

One landed on the red drop and began to eat. Everyone stood, silent. Melissa edged toward the man, so she could see. The bee lifted from his finger like a tiny helicopter. Where it had been, she saw a round, white spot—perfectly clean.

It seemed to her that all the voices were screaming, making a wall of noise so thick, she couldn't make them out. She held out her hand. Against the black hand of the homeless man, hers was so small and new. He spooned jam onto the tip of her finger, and she stretched it out over the table. Another bee landed, and she shivered at the tiny lightness on her skin.

"Only yellow jackets," the man said. "Hungry." His real voice was so much different. Unused, but the voice of an ordinary man. "Won't hurt you," he said.

She watched the yellow jacket lift from her finger. When she turned back, the man stood listening, then jerked his head from side to side, as if he had something lodged in his ear. He searched the trees and bushes around them, and his whole body began to shiver. Desperate, he looked at Melissa, as if she could help.

Without thinking, she slid a laden plate from the table and lifted the white cloth.

"Here," she said. "In here."

The man didn't hesitate. He ducked under the table, and Melissa pushed the plate ahead and crawled in after him. He sat cross-legged, shivering, one hand on his head for protection, and Melissa sat in her party dress, her knees pressed into her chin. She heard her mother and father rush forward, embarrassed and afraid, asking their guests what they should do. But Melissa wasn't moving. Not until the coast was clear.

ZOO

On the day she was fired, it was raining, a rare spring rain in southern California. The streets ran like rivers, and cars, though they crept through intersections, sent arcing waves of water over the curbs. Clouds descended on dry hills in billows of blue and gray, and in between, shafts of yellow sunlight turned the blank, dirty buildings new again. Mirna rolled down the windows and let the coolness sweep through her car. She accelerated onto the freeway for the long drive home. Near her apartment in Santa Monica, she exited the freeway and stopped at the corner market to load her trunk and backseat with nested liquor boxes.

"There is wealth in empty boxes," she thought. She made several trips from the car to her apartment and placed the boxes at intervals on the carpet in her living room before she began to remove her books from their shelves, one by one. She dusted each volume and set it in the nearest box. She stopped to shove open the bottoms of the windows and let the cool air in. It tingled on her skin and curled her hair.

She brewed a pot of coffee and continued. Near sunset, she retrieved three boxes of journals from the bottom of her closet, journals she'd been keeping since she was a girl. Gradually, her perfect schoolgirl script had deteriorated, her letters growing large and uneven. The first years were recorded in dusty steno notebooks, filled with random dreams, short poems, and quotations from the books she'd read. Reading ahead, she was struck by a few lines from Sartre on what a shame it is that we all live our lives from the outside.

"What if we don't?" she thought. In the years of journals, she found nothing to tell her what her life had been. Nothing to remind her of her joys and of her sadnesses. She had recorded every fight she'd had with her mother. Every lover who had let her down. But nothing, anywhere, about her job.

Nothing about Tony, who when he was twelve had blocked her path as she walked across the patio on her way to class, sleep deprived, exhausted, filled with dread. He had swept before her, flinging about him a swirling black cape, and for no reason thrown himself to one knee and belted out "Don't Cry for Me, Argentina." She had stopped still and laughed, delighted beyond measure. Later, and despite all her effort, Tony was expelled.

There was nothing in her journal about the day she'd walked into her tenth-grade English class and found all the students crouched on the carpet in one corner . . . playing on her something like a visual joke. She had joined them and conducted the entire class from the floor. No one ever mentioned it.

She'd never written about Jonah, a transfer student who had spent two years at the school "holding up a wall." She often saw him, tall and winsome, standing alone, leaning against a building. He seldom spoke. But years after graduation, years after he silently occupied a seat in the back row of

her class, he appeared after school to show her a film, a film
he'd animated with clay figures and crinkled tinfoil, depicting the sweet and silly domesticity of Adam and Eve from
Paradise Lost—Eve, beguiled by the serpent, and Adam,
undone and whining. Though the film had earned him a
place in a famous film school, she knew he had made it for
her. Only she would see its depth of innocence and charm.

Why hadn't she written these things down? How could
she, in all these years, not have known this was her life? It
had partly been because nobody wants to talk to schoolteachers. At parties in Los Angeles, she was introduced to lawyers
and artists, actors and agents. When she told them what she
did, it was almost as if a curtain drifted down. The change
was subtle, but conversation stalled. Men, especially, gazed
beyond her, even as she spoke. She joked to herself that she
was becoming an old-maid schoolteacher, but she also
thought, "This must be how mothers, locked away with
small children, begin to feel. Invisible."

Each weekday she drove from Santa Monica, more than
an hour each way to school, leaving just at seven in the
morning, and finding back roads through Beverly Hills and

her class, he appeared after school to show her a film, a film he'd animated with clay figures and crinkled tinfoil, depicting the sweet and silly domesticity of Adam and Eve from *Paradise Lost*—Eve, beguiled by the serpent, and Adam, undone and whining. Though the film had earned him a place in a famous film school, she knew he had made it for her. Only she would see its depth of innocence and charm.

Why hadn't she written these things down? How could she, in all these years, not have known this was her life? It had partly been because nobody wants to talk to schoolteachers. At parties in Los Angeles, she was introduced to lawyers and artists, actors and agents. When she told them what she did, it was almost as if a curtain drifted down. The change was subtle, but conversation stalled. Men, especially, gazed beyond her, even as she spoke. She joked to herself that she was becoming an old-maid schoolteacher, but she also thought, "This must be how mothers, locked away with small children, begin to feel. Invisible."

Each weekday she drove from Santa Monica, more than an hour each way to school, leaving just at seven in the morning, and finding back roads through Beverly Hills and

Brentwood. It seemed that every car she saw was a new, glistening black Mercedes or BMW. It began to seem to her that she was poor, and always would be. How could her students, who also drove expensive cars, respect her? How could she recommend an academic life? How would her best students, so unprepared, survive in the world?

At graduation that year, her favorite students, who mocked the new headmistress behind her back, grasped their rolled diplomas and embraced the plump, gray-haired woman in expansive hugs. As Mirna sat in the darkened auditorium, the class exited down the aisle, like crows, exultant, lifting from the trees. They raced down the aisle to pounding music: "You Can Get It If You Really Try." Mirna sat alone in her chair, forgotten. After the ceremony, the graduates hovered close to their suddenly enlarged families, like goslings jostling for a place under the wing. They went on to parties or out to dinner—they went on to "real life." She drove home alone.

Then back to school for an entire week of meetings. She sat with all the weary faculty in the stifling-hot library, where the headmistress insisted that they autopsy the year behind and plan the year to come. Exhausted, the

Due to a printer's error,

page 212 was omitted from the first printing of

Christina Adam's *Any Small Thing Can Save You.*

We provide this erratum to complete the edition.

faculty adhered to an unspoken pact: Keep quiet, don't talk, get it over with. It was the meetings that had ended it for her.

In the last few months, students from the public school had drifted down the street and picked fights with their senior boys. Mirna had been walking to her parked car when she heard angry voices. She turned and ran toward a group of shoving boys and watching girls. In the center, two boys fought. It was nothing like a fight on television or in a movie. Adrenaline and fear stung in the air, and the sound of a fist striking flesh was a sound she would never forget. The sight of blood, a split eyebrow, felt like a blow to her own flesh. She had been surprised at her courage in the face not only of the trespasser, but of her own student, who shook with fear and rage, tears tracking dirt and blood down his cheeks, when she pulled him away.

These events were at the top of the headmistress's list. She had decided to arm the janitor, a former policeman, and use him as a guard—when he wasn't fixing plumbing. Mirna was the only teacher to challenge her. She had had dealings with the janitor, a self-important, stupid man who hoarded keys and enforced parking rules. She looked at the impassive faces of her colleagues—educated people, many of them Ph.D.s. What were they thinking?

The headmistress raised her voice and commanded Mirna to be quiet. But Mirna kept on pushing, her voice lifting, growing strident. "You have a gun, somebody will be *shot*," she said. "Statistics *prove* that."

"Shut up," the headmistress said. Shocked, the faculty stared. Mirna looked at them again. Why were they silent?

Mirna slid out of her student chair. "No," she said. Her chairman put a hand on her elbow. She shook him off. "You think the janitor should shoot a child?"

"We will discuss this at *another* time," the headmistress said, but her voice quavered as if with fear.

Mirna thought, "She's going to crack." She knew she should back down, but she couldn't stop herself. "You bring a gun in here, I'm leaving," she said.

The older woman gripped the arms of her chair. "I'll have you fired," she said.

The room seemed to empty of air.

. . .

Mirna might have fought the board's decision. She might have phoned one of the lawyers who refused to speak to her at parties. She might have called parents and students, raised a groundswell of support.

Instead, she went on packing. From time to time during the night, she opened another journal. Ten years she had taught at this school, her meager salary growing slowly to the point that just this year she'd made enough to save, enough to weather a small emergency, a car repair or dental work.

The school had changed. The times had changed. "Perhaps," she thought, "I've stayed too long." In the first years she taught, the students, though they didn't know it, ran the school. They planned their own assemblies and art fairs. One year, Mirna had arrived in the early morning to find the parking lot barricaded with sawhorses and the students in camouflage lofting toy machine guns. It was May Day. She suffered a mock search and interrogation and drove into the lot, where students stood on platforms making speeches through bullhorns. Later that morning, Mirna had a meeting with a visitor from a prestigious private school for girls. Good-humored, he had merely commented, "Where

I came from this morning, they were tying ribbons on Maypoles."

The new headmistress, a former nun, was more interested in courting favor with the board of directors, in raising money and perfecting her own image, than she was in children. It had taken Mirna a long time to understand how people like ministers and headmistresses could seem so concerned, so earnest, and still make her skin crawl. She emptied a box she had already packed and lifted out a slim black and yellow paperback. T. S. Eliot, *The Cocktail Party*. The lines would be in her journals somewhere, but just now, it was easier to find the book itself.

> *Half the harm that is done in this world*
> *Is due to people who want to feel important.*
> *They don't mean to do harm—but the harm does not*
> *   interest them.*
> *Or they do not see it, or they justify it*
> *Because they are absorbed in the endless struggle*
> *To think well of themselves.*

T. S. Eliot, she recalled, taught high school. She wondered if he had noticed how each class, if they stayed
together from grade school, formed a group personality. Her
tenth-grade class that year had been so driven, so ruthless
and competitive, most of the girls had dropped out along the
way. The remaining boys were good students, if anxious and
unkind. They would do what it took to please her—if it got
them into the right schools.

But once, it had been different. She spread the journals
out on the carpet and looked for the right year. When she
found it, she scanned every entry. Nowhere had she mentioned anything about Katherine, Will, Angelique, or Raye.

These had been young star students when she'd first
taken the job. They performed in plays and art fairs, led
the mock revolution, and held debates—in full costume—
between Golda Meir and Yasir Arafat. They were beautiful
children whom *the faculty* had envied and admired. Mirna
could remember overhearing the old headmaster say of
Katherine, "You watch, we're going to see her face on the
cover of *Time*."

Though in awe herself, Mirna loved them because they
were smart. For the first time since she had left college, she

found herself entranced with thinking, with ideas. They read Genesis, *Canterbury Tales,* and *Hamlet.* They talked about Milton, Henry James, and Beckett. They rode the train to the zoo.

It began on a morning break as they were standing in the parking lot—a plan to take the train to San Diego, to the zoo. They joked about holding a bake sale to raise their train fares. "Do it with pot brownies . . . and *maybe* we can make enough."

But each one came up with the money. They met downtown at the train station, a place she had never been, and rode through the switching yards into the secret center of L.A. This is what they wanted her to see. Round storage tanks painted sky blue, yellow, primrose pink. Smokestacks and pyramids of blue-green, shattered glass that glistened in the sun like glacial ice. They passed yards filled with bricks and tile and turquoise plastic pipe. Miles of peeling, colored barrels, stacked like crayons new inside the box.

From this, the train burst upon the ocean and kept it close along one side. They could see the surf break on the sand. Katherine was so tall, she seemed to have to bend to walk along the aisle. She wore a teal-colored cotton sweater Mirna had never seen, a new sweater. It made her eyes appear so blue, Mirna found herself looking away. Katherine seemed not to know how beautiful she was. Will lounged with his long, white legs dangling over the arm of his seat, so easy in his body and so young.

Though Mirna was barely twenty-five, they sometimes left her feeling ancient. She had grown up with none of the recognition these kids had—none of the appreciation, the warmth, the opportunities. Though she was attractive, she had never thought herself beautiful. It wasn't until she taught her first class at the school that she looked at the smooth, pale faces around the table and understood: All healthy children are lovely. It would be so good if they could know it.

Angelique giggled. She looked like a figure from a Reubens painting, not plump, but rounded and easily blush-ing. The most unlikely things made her blush and laugh—moments of folly in the world that anyone else would miss. And Raye, dressed in black, her dark hair clipped close; the politician in the group, the moral voice.

They led her through the San Diego Zoo. They had planned to draw, but only Will sat down on the curb in front of the zebras. Mirna looked at zebras as if for the first time. Somehow in her mind, they had seemed painted with stripes. Now she saw how each hair was either black or brown or white, how unlike horses they were. How impossible to imagine or recreate.

Ducks and exotic fowl wandered, loose, along the paths. Angelique couldn't get over the ducks. Whatever it was inside of her that found so many things embarrassing and funny was drawn to ducks. *Beaks* struck her as funny. She sat down and painted *beaks.*

Katherine walked through the scattered crowd unaware that people stopped to stare at her as if another exotic bird had alighted among them. She was the only one who had no college plans. All her teachers had argued with her, but she remained, as always, solitary and steady on her way. She would be an actress.

Raye walked with Mirna. They made a point of hiking up to the wolf pens, of finding the giraffes and polar bears, but they spent the most time in the cool dark of the reptile house, marveling at animals that came in neon blue and tender green. They studied crimson and yellow frogs, striped snakes, and goggle-eyed chameleons.

The time was so near graduation, Raye began to try to shock her, telling her about the days when half the class was stoned. Who slept with whom, students and faculty. Mirna rolled her eyes. Where had she been? She knew these students so well. She knew how their minds worked, what made them laugh, and what they feared. Yet, she knew them not at all.

The day Mirna was fired, all those students, except Katherine, had graduated from college. Katherine was a movie star. Her face had not appeared on the cover of *Time*, but on *Newsweek*. From time to time, they sent her marvelous postcards, Will's with postage stamps—of mountain goats, gazelles, past presidents—drawn on beside the real ones.

She thought of them in their young lives and stood up from the floor. Her knees and ankles ached from sitting. She looked around her living room. There was a painting Will had given her, a stack of photographs from Raye, and a dozen small paintings of ducks, yellow ducks, from Angelique. She packed them in a dress box and carried it out to the car.

Past midnight, she could smell the rain and the salt air from the ocean. What she had come to love about Santa Monica was the light, the pale-blue light that fell on ugly, angular, post-war buildings and turned them shades of gold. But lately, her life had been stacks of unmarked student papers, messages to call unhappy parents, books unread and piled up on the floor.

She carried boxes of books and journals, her clothes, and her bedding out to the curb and filled the trunk and backseat of her car. Her furniture could go back to the Salvation Army, where it had come from in the first place. She left a note on the landlord's door, "Leaving. You have my deposit."

"Something about being fired," she thought, "keeps you wide awake." There was barely room for her to slide into the driver's seat, pull her elbow in, and slam the door. She rolled down the window. Rain fell, but lightly.

She negotiated the dark residential streets and drove too fast up the sweeping ramp of the freeway. The small car slipped sideways, hydroplaning on the oil-slick surface. She eased into a lane and gripped the wheel, her shoulders stiff with fear.

"Where are you going?" she said to herself.

When her heartbeat steadied, she thought, "We all want to think well of ourselves. We think we are doing no harm, but we are all afraid." She had spent ten years shepherding others toward their dreams. But she had been ashamed— because she was afraid of her own.

The freeway ended at the ocean, and she had to make a choice. She had to turn, north or south. She drove along the ocean, north past Malibu. She thought about Huck Finn, lighting out for the territories. But she had already reached the edge of North America. A round moon rose over the hills, and black water glistened on the road, a road so empty, she could hear waves crashing on the shore. She could hear each separate wave, the lunar pull against the turning of the earth, the continent colliding with the sea.

ACKNOWLEDGMENTS

It is my great pleasure to acknowledge publicly all those who with their support and encouragement have, through the fullness of time, made this book possible, especially: Don Watson, Rick and Pat Adam, Jean Adam, Mimi Seawell, Geoff Adam, John Adam, Connie Brown, Joan Koyen, C. Michael Curtis, Michael Enright, Stefanie Herzstein, Martha Hipp, Camden Morse, Judith Slater, Jan Swindlehurst, Bernadette Valdez, Luella D. Watson, and the Idaho Commission on the Arts.

For their hospitality, aid, and comfort during the writing of this book, I am grateful to Nick, Ron, and Lina Erin, and I am especially grateful for the insights of Katherine McGovern, Marjorie Rommel, and Selma Moskowitz, the brightest and best, who read this book in manuscript.

At BlueHen Books, I want to acknowledge the work and enthusiasm of Caitlin Hamilton and Kim Frederick-Law, and the talent, care, and inimitable good taste of Fred Ramey, the gentleman editor. No book could have been in better hands.

For his wisdom, kindness, and diligence, I will always be grateful to my agent, Charles Everitt.

I also want to thank the students I've been privileged to teach, and my friends and neighbors in Idaho and New Mexico—for telling me stories and always being ready to come to the rescue—particularly Tom Schmid, Joanie Ericson, and Cicero and Duane and Jean Kunz and their family.

Finally, I want to acknowledge the generosity and integrity of Dianne Benedict and Mark Doty, who, by example, keep reminding me that language can transform the world.